**SELECTED STORIES OF
E.W. THOMSON**

Cover illustration by Douglas A. Fales

SELECTED STORIES OF

E.W. THOMSON

Edited and with an Introduction

by

LORRAINE MCMULLEN

University of Ottawa Press
Ottawa, Canada
1973

Canadian Short Stories series
of the
Department of English, University of Ottawa
No. 3

Glenn Clever, General Editor

Volumes published to date:

No. 1 Selected Stories of Duncan Campbell Scott, ed. Glenn Clever
No. 2 Selected Stories of Raymond Knister, ed. Michael Gnarowski

PREFATORY NOTE

I would like to acknowledge the support and interest of Professor Michael Gnarowski, Carleton University, and Professor Glenn Clever, University of Ottawa.

The stories included here were published in *Old Man Savarin and Other Stories*, Toronto, William Briggs, 1895, with the exception of "Dour Davie's Drive" published in *Between Earth and Sky, and Other Strange Stories of Deliverance*, Toronto, William Briggs, 1897, and "Miss Minnely's Management" published in *University Magazine*, Montreal. All were republished in *Old Man Savarin Stories*, Toronto, S.B. Gundy, 1917.

Every reasonable care has been taken to trace the copyright ownership of this material. The editor and publisher will welcome information on copyright ownership.

L.M.

TABLE OF CONTENTS

PAGE

Prefatory Note vii
Introduction xi

Old Man Savarin 1
McGrath's Bad Night 9
Privilege of the Limits 17
Great Godfreys's Lament 23
Dour Davie's Drive 31
Red-Headed Windego 39
Little Baptiste – Ottawa River 47
The Waterloo Veteran 57
The Ride by Night 61
"Drafted" 69
Miss Mennely's Management 77

The Author 89
Selected Bibliography 91

INTRODUCTION

Increased literary activity in Canada after Confederation paralleled a growing sense of national pride and an awareness of the need for a national culture. Although poetry replaced prose as the dominant mode of literary expression, a considerable body of prose fiction was produced. A number of magazines were founded: *The Canadian Monthly and National Review* in 1872, *The Nation* in 1874, and *The Week,* the most outstanding journal of its time, in 1883. These, along with American periodicals, provided outlets for the Canadian writer. The most popular form of fiction was the historical romance, celebrating Canadian heroes of the past, or using a historical setting, most often the French Canadian setting and past, for sensational romantic tales.

Edward William Thomson (1849-1924) was the most skilful Canadian story teller of the time. He was at once a part of his age and distinct from it. Thomson's best stories have the local colour of the Glengarry and Ottawa River settings and at the same time show an awareness of realism which is not at all evident in other Canadian writers of that time. In fact, with the exception of Thomson, realism was not to have a significant impact on Canadian writing for some time to come. Canadian reaction to realism is noted by Desmond Pacey in *Creative Writing in Canada*, "Reviews in *The Week* referred with undisguised horror to 'the intellectual vivisection methods of the American schools of James and Howells, or, worse still, the loathsome realism and putridity of the school of Zola and France!' " These remarks are not altogether surprising in light of the controversy over realism then taking place in literary journals in England. Among the most notable participants in this controversy were Arthur Waugh writing in *The Yellow Book* 1894 and Havelock Ellis in *The Savoy* 1896.[1]

Because Thomson had read and admired many of the European realists, their influence is evident in his stories. Thomson's Canada

[1]In the first issue of *The Yellow Book* (April, 1894), Arthur Waugh, father of Evelyn the novelist, attacked realistic fiction which had its beginnings on the continent and at that time was becoming apparent in England, "A new school has arisen which combines the characteristics of effeminancy and brutality. In its effeminate aspect it plays with the subtler emotion of sensual pleasure, in its brutal it has developed into that class of fiction which for want of a better word I must call chirurgical...." Waugh recommended that "The standard of taste in literature...steer a middle course between the prudery of the manse which is for hiding everything vital and the effrontery of the pot-house, which makes for ribaldry and bawdry". The second issue of *The Yellow Book* (July 1894) continued the debate, with the short story writer Hubert Crackenthorpe supporting realistic fiction and Philip Gilbert Hamerton agreeing with Waugh, though finding his arguments inadequate. When *The Savoy* began publication in 1896 the discussion continued. In the first issue Havelock Ellis in an article on Zola said, "In every civilized country we have heard of the man who has dragged literature into the gutter, who has gone down to pick up the filth of the streets, and has put it into books for the filthy to read...in England, the classic land of self-righteousness, the decree went forth that this thing must be put an end to, and amid general acclamation the English publisher of such garbage was slapped into gaol."

is that of the pioneers, and he presents realistic portraits of woodsmen, farmers, and store-keepers based on close observation of life
and a genuine love of the common man. However, the happy endings
of most of his stories and the sentimentality of some are not consistent with realism, but show that Thomson shares with his age a
tendency to romance. Nor does Thomson suggest any of the moral
permissiveness or exploration of sex characteristic of some of the
European writers he admired. He is closer to realism as practised in
England than to such European models as Zola and Maupassant.

The varied experiences of his own life provided Thomson with
considerable material for fiction. One of the most memorable incidents
of his boyhood was a brief, accidental meeting with Abraham Lincoln.
Thomson, visiting an uncle in Philadelphia, was standing in front of
a store when a tall, impressive looking man stopped and spoke to him.
Young Thomson, who was fourteen years of age at the time, recognized
the man as Abraham Lincoln. Lincoln remained one of his great heroes,
and a number of poems in his praise are found in Thomson's collection
of poetry, *The Many-Mansioned House and Other Poems*. The American edition of these poems was titled *When Lincoln Died and Other
Poems*.

Thomson's experiences in the American Civil War provided
material for a number of stories, of which "Drafted" and "The Ride
by Night" appear in this selection. In October 1864, during a visit to
the United States, he enlisted in the Third Pennsylvania Cavalry. He
saw action at Hatcher's Run and served with General Grant at Peters-
burg. Because he was only fifteen, his parents were able to obtain his
release from the army in 1865. He was home only a year when another
opportunity for action presented itself, and he enlisted in the Queen's
Own Rifles to fight the Fenians.

After this second adventure in soldiering, the young man settled
down to study civil engineering and surveying, and from 1872 to 1878
worked as a land surveyor for railway and lumbering operations in
eastern Ontario. The experiences and acquaintances of these years
bore fruit in some of his best stories, of the French, Irish, and Scottish
settlers along the Ottawa River. In 1873, while working on the building
of the Carillon canal, Thomson met and married Adelaide St. Denis,
daughter of Alexandre St. Denis, a wealthy merchant of Point Fortune.
St. Denis seems to have disapproved of the match. Arthur S. Bourinot
quotes a 1957 newspaper review of a book about the area to the effect
that local tradition reports the marriage an elopement.[2]

In December 1878 Thomson joined the Toronto *Globe* as an
editorial writer. For two years, 1882 to 1883, he returned to land surveying, this time at Winnipeg during the real estate boom which resulted
from the opening up of the west by the railway. Except for this period
he remained with the *Globe* until 1891. Thomson was a skilful, eloquent,

[2]Julia Grace Wales, "An Experience Rich in Color and Character of Carillon-Point
Fortune Neighbourhood". Book review in *The Lachute Watchman*, Jan. 24, 1957,
quoted in Arthur S. Bourinot, ed., *The Letters of Edward William Thomson to Archibald
Lampman (1891-1897)*, p. 29.

and uncompromising journalist much involved with political concerns of the day. Such political involvement came naturally to him. There were politicians on both sides of the family. His mother's brother, the Honourable M.H. Foley, had been Postmaster-General of Canada before Confederation. His grandfather, Colonel Edward Thomson, had been a member of the Upper Canada Legislature, and in 1836 had defeated William Lyon Mackenzie in a York election. Thomson's reason for leaving the *Globe* in 1891 was, not surprisingly, a political one, his disagreement with the Liberal party's campaign based on the issue of "unrestricted reciprocity."[3]

Thomson then accepted a position as revising editor for *Youth's Companion*, a boys' magazine published in Boston. His first contact with this magazine had occurred some years earlier; in 1885 he had entered a short story competition held by *Youth's Companion* and won the first prize of five hundred dollars for "Petherick's Peril", a story published in *Between Earth and Sky, and Other Strange Stories of Deliverance* (1897) and in *Old Man Savarin Stories* (1917). Thomson spent ten years in Boston. His position does not seem to have been as demanding as the physically rugged surveying or the intellectually strenuous journalism of his earlier years. At one time Thomson wrote to Archibald Lampman suggesting he consider a position as reader for the magazine, a major reason for recommending this position being that readers had "solid chunks of leisure," extremely helpful, of course, for the creative writer. These Boston years were undoubtedly Thomson's most prolific as a writer of prose fiction. During this time he published his fine collection of short stories, *Old Man Savarin and Other Stories* (1895), and also *Smoky Days* (1896), a boys' adventure story, and two collections of stories for boys: *Walter Gibbs, The Young Boss; and Other Stories* (1896), *Between Earth and Sky, and Other Strange Stories of Deliverance* (1897). Many of the stories in these collections had appeared earlier in *Youth's Companion*. Thomson based several short stories on his Boston experiences. The most amusing of these, "Miss Minnely's Management," appears in this volume. It is a satire of Thomson's own occupation of revising stories to make them suitable for the tender ears of *Youth's Companion* readers.

While living in the United States, Thomson remained in touch with his Canadian friends and made frequent trips to Canada. His exchange of letters with Lampman indicates the warmth of their friendship and Thomson's continued interest in the Canadian literary scene. In 1901 he returned to Canada. He spent a year with the Montreal *Star* before accepting the position he was to hold for twenty years as Canadian correspondent of the *Boston Transcript*. Thomson

[3]The Liberal party under the leadership of Wilfred Laurier had advocated complete removal of tariffs between Canada and the United States, and fought the 1891 election campaign on this issue of "unrestricted reciprocity". Sir John A. Macdonald, Prime Minister and leader of the Conservative party, argued that this form of commercial union would lead eventually to political union and based his electoral campaign on the issue of Canadian independence in North America. Macdonald won the election. Many Liberal supporters could not endorse Laurier's stand; among them was Thomson. Thus he resigned as editorial writer for the strongly Liberal Toronto *Globe*.

now lived in Ottawa, where he was accepted as a major figure on the literary and political scene. He was a close friend of two major Canadian statesmen of the day, Sir Wilfred Laurier and Henri Bourassa. That Thomson was an astute political observer and adviser is indicated by Laurier's recommendation of him to the South African government as a constitutional adviser following the Boer war. During his years in Ottawa, Thomson found time to publish his one volume of poetry, which contains a number of narrative poems of Canada and the United States and personal reminiscences of the American Civil War. He re-published his *Old Man Savarin* stories in 1917, the new volume containing twelve of the original fourteen *Old Man Savarin* stories and five additional stories, two of which had been published in *Between Earth and Sky, and Other Strange Stories of Deliverance.*

Thomson remained active as correspondent for the *Boston Transcript* into his seventies. He died in Boston on March 5, 1924.

Of the stories in this selection, eight are set in Canada, two deal with the American Civil War, and one deals with an American publishing company. Thomson admired Emile Zola, William Dean Howells and Henry James, and was alone in Canada in applying a realistic approach to the Canadian setting and characters. He presents a view of life in early Canadian settlements that is lively, energetic, and entertaining. That it is also authentic stems from the fact that Thomson's own experiences provided much of the material for his stories. Some of the incidents described are humorous, some sentimental, and some a mixture of the two.

Thomson's sympathies are obviously with the common man. His heroes are woodsmen, hewers, teamsters in the lumber camps, farmers, fish peddlers—all simple, likeable human beings. Thomson has remarked in his letters his genuine interest in all men, in elevator boys and office cleaners as well as in "people who despise me for these associations." Writing to Archibald Lampman, August 13, 1896, Thomson said, in reference to literary men, "None of them are as interesting as lumbermen, farmers, tailors, the entire class of *Moujiks*—from whom one [who] gives them sympathy can gain more information about its movement in the human breast than from any sort of writing people."

Most of the stories focus on the characters: Mr. McTavish, the Glengarry Scotsman who finds himself in prison for debt; Narcisse Larocque who loses his fishing platform; Peter McGrath, the unemployed labourer who resorts to stealing food for his family of eleven; old John the Waterloo veteran turned fish pedlar who "called 'Fresh white-fish' as if calling all the village to fall in for drill." All are very human—they drink, swear, fight, and steal. But they are kind, hardworking, vigorous, and independent—a hardy pioneer stock. The outstanding characteristic of Thomson's pioneers is their stubbornness. Larocque insists on his right to continue fishing from the platform, and the new landowner is equally insistent that he pay rent for the privilege; McTavish refuses to pay a debt he is convinced is not due, and Tougal Stewart just as stubbornly pays three times the money McTavish owes him to keep him in prison for non-payment; Davie McAndrew stubbornly insists on making a three-day trip through the winter bush alone, despite a broken leg.

Thomson's villain is most often the only prosperous person in the story, the village storekeeper. McGrath's family goes hungry because there is no credit at the village store for the unemployed. The destitute family of Baptiste Larocque is threatened with eviction by John Connolly, owner of the store, the tavern, and the sawmill, who is described as "the vampire of the little hamlet". Narcisse Larocque is refused entry to the land on which his fishing platform is built by Old Man Savarin, the storekeeper.

None of the stories contains a romantic love interest in the traditional sense, nor is there any theme of sex which was then becoming so popular with European writers. The central characters are vigourously masculine—several stories concern the all-male world of the army or the lumber camp. Although Thomson's female characters are generally neither strongly developed nor much in evidence, there are two young women who stand out in "Old Man Savarin". Ma'am Paradis tells how, as a fifteen-year old, with her seventeen-year old cousin Alphonsine Seguin, she outwits Old Man Savarin. Both young girls demonstrate the initiative and quick wit characteristic of most of Thomson's male characters. The fifteen-year old says to Savarin as she is about to pull him out of the river, "What you goin' pay for all dat? You tink I'll be goin' for mos' kill myself pullin' you out for noting? When you ever do someting for anybody for noting, eh, M'sieu Savarin?" Another remarkable female character is the redoubtable Miss Minnely of "Miss Minnely's Management". Owner of *The Family Blessing*, Miss Minnely turns the tables on *The Family Blessing's* derider and leaves that gentleman wondering if she can possibly be as ingenuous as she appears or is a skilful manipulator. With the exception of these two stories, women tend to remain in the background; for example, Mary Ann McGrath and Delima Larocque are patient and longsuffering mothers of large families who wait for husband or son to solve the problems attendant upon their poverty.

In most stories description is minimal yet is sufficient to lend an air of reality. Thomson is apt in his use of colourful similes which grow naturally out of situation and setting. Mrs. McGrath assesses her lumberman husband's stubbornness, "Mary Ann knew that she might as well try to convince a saw-log to go upstream as to protest against Peter's obstinancy." We are told that Old John, the Waterloo veteran, serves out his fish "with an air of distributing ammunition for a long day's combat." Godfrey's Indian mother is described as "brown as November oak leaves," and Godfrey "white that day as the froth on the rapid," with blue eyes that "would match the sky when you'll be seeing it up through a blazing maple on a clear day of October."

Dialogue is used skilfully. Some stories are given a conversational frame; a participant or observer relates the events to a second person. This narrative method is used in "Privilege of the Limits", "Old

Man Savarin", "Great Godfrey's Lament", and "The Ride by Night". Thus an informal, conversational style is achieved with a first-person narrative. Scottish and French Canadian characters use dialect and a few French words are interspersed by French Canadian speakers to contribute to the impression of reality. During the eighteen-nineties dialect was becoming increasingly popular in British fiction with the Scottish dialect of J.M. Barrie's stories and the prevalence of Irish and Cockney dialect in much realistic fiction. Thomson parallels his British colleagues in this particular aspect of realism.

All of the stories convey a sense of immediacy. "Old Man Savarin" is a first-person narrative in which the entire tale is presented by Ma'am Paradis who gives a verbatim account of conversations from the past. We, as readers, are made to feel that we are really there by the water's edge, listening to the old lady as she sits smoking her clay pipe and saying, "Then you hain't nev' hear 'bout the old time Old Man Savarin was catched up with. No, eh? Well, I'll tol' you 'bout that." Transitions are made naturally and casually by the interjection of the occasional question which leads Ma'am Paradis on from one incident to the next in her story.

"Red-Headed Windego" plunges us immediately into a third-person narrative, with necessary background filled in as the story proceeds. A surveying crew is attempting to run a line around a disputed timber area to secure the claim for their employer. A rival contrives to frighten the crew by making giant tracks across the snow, seemingly the tracks of a Windego. The crew, most of whom have some Indian blood, believe in the legend of the monstrous Windego, a being that can take any shape or size to lure men to their doom. The story focuses on the young surveyor's attempt to outwit the "Windego" and get his frightened crew back to work. The story contains a precise and accurate picture of the surveying operation. What a hardy breed were these men! Working all winter, they carried "light" forty pound packs, strode through the forest on six-foot snow-shoes, lunched on cold pork and hard-tack, and slept under an open tent pitched over a hole in the snow. The narrative itself is never static; it moves quickly, keeping description of both character and scenery to a minimum. Yet despite this economy we are given a vivid picture of this particular aspect of early Canadian life.

Very different in theme is the one story set in an American publishing house. Thomson does not waste words but launches immediately into satire with the first sentence: "George Renwick substituted 'limb' for 'leg', 'intoxicated' for 'drunk', and 'undergarment' for 'shirt' in 'The Converted Ringmaster', a short-story-of-commerce which he was editing for *The Family Blessing*. When he should have eliminated all indecorum it would go to Miss Minnely, who would 'elevate the emotional interest.' "

Of the two Civil War stories, "The Ride by Night" is most notable for its rapid action and the atmosphere of urgency developed and sustained throughout the narrative. "Drafted" relates the unhappy meeting of two young brothers as one is dying on the battlefield. In its emotional presentation of the meeting of a young Union soldier with his dying brother, a Confederate draftee, this is the most sentimental of the stories in this selection. Setting is more fully described than usual; here Thomson demonstrates his descriptive powers in his bleak picture of the miserable camp life of the young soldier and the sounds of the distant battle. In both of these war stories the protagonists are very young men, Thomson apparently portraying events as they had existed for him as a fifteen-year old soldier.

Despite the skill evident in these latter stories, the authenticity of the Canadian pioneer life and pioneer characters remains the main source of interest in Thomson's stories; he gives an insight into the difficult life and tenacious spirit of the lumberman, teamster, farmer —for whom even a frugal life demanded courage, hard work, and determination. Contributing also in no small measure to the effectiveness of his stories are Thomson's humour and his ability to create sharply memorable characters.

Lorraine McMullen
University of Ottawa

Old Man Savarin

Old Ma'ame Paradis had caught seventeen small doré, four suckers, and eleven channel-catfish before she used up all the worms in her tomato-can. Therefore she was in a cheerful and loquacious humor when I came along and offered her some of my bait.

"Merci; non, M'sieu. Dat's 'nuff fishin' for me. I got too old now for fish too much. You like me make you present of six or seven doré? Yes? All right. Then you make me present of one quarter dollar."

When this transaction was completed, the old lady got out her short black clay pipe, and filled it with *tabac blanc*.

"Ver' good smell for scare mosquitoes," said she. "Sit down, M'sieu. For sure I like to be here, me, for see the river when she's like this."

Indeed the scene was more than picturesque. Her fishing-platform extended twenty feet from the rocky shore of the great Rataplan Rapid of the Ottawa, which, beginning to tumble a mile to the westward, poured a roaring torrent half a mile wide into the broader, calm brown reach below. Noble elms towered on the shores. Between their trunks we could see many whitewashed cabins, whose doors of blue or green or red scarcely disclosed their colors in that light.

The sinking sun, which already touched the river, seemed somehow the source of the vast stream that flowed radiantly from its blaze. Through the glamour of the evening mist and the maze of June flies we could see a dozen men scooping for fish from platforms like that of Ma'ame Paradis.

Each scooper lifted a great hoop-net set on a handle some fifteen feet long, threw it easily up stream, and swept it on edge with the current to the full length of his reach. Then it was drawn out and at once thrown upward again, if no capture had been made. In case he had taken fish, he came to the inshore edge of his platform, and upset the net's contents into a pool separated from the main rapid by an improvised wall of stones.

"I'm too old for scoop some now," said Ma'ame Paradis, with a sigh.

"You were never strong enough to scoop, surely," said I.

"No, eh? All right, M'sieu. Then you hain't nev' hear 'bout the time Old Man Savarin was catched up with. No, eh? Well, I'll tol' you 'bout that." And this was her story as she told it to me.

"Der was fun dose time. Nobody ain't nev' catch up with dat old rascal any other time since I'll know him first. Me, I'll be only fifteen den. Dat's long time 'go, eh? Well, for sure, I ain't so old like what I'll look. But Old Man Savarin was old already. He's old, old, old,

when he's only thirty; an' *mean—baptême!* If de old Nick ain' got de
hottest place for dat old stingy—yes, for sure!

"You'll see up dere where Frawce Seguin is scoop? Dat's the
Laroque platform by right. Me, I was a Laroque. My fader was use for
scoop dere, an' my gran'fader—the Laroques scoop dere all de time since
ever dere was some Rapid Rataplan. Den Old Man Savarin he's buyed
the land up dere from Felix Ladoucier, an' he's told my fader, 'You can't
scoop no more wisout you pay me rent.'

" 'Rent!' my fader say. '*Saprie!* Dat's my fader's platform for
scoop fish! You ask anybody.'

" 'Oh, I'll know all 'bout dat,' Old Man Savarin is say. 'Ladoucier
let you scoop front of his land, for Ladoucier one big fool. De lan's
mine now, an' de fishin' right is mine. You can't scoop dere wisout
you pay me rent.'

" '*Baptême!* I'll show you 'bout dat,' my fader say.

"Next mawny he is go for scoop same like always. Den Old Man
Savarin is fetch my fader up before de magistrate. De magistrate make
my fader pay nine shillin'!

" 'Mebbe dat's learn you one lesson,' Old Man Savarin is say.

"My fader swear pretty good, but my moder say: 'Well, Narcisse,
dere hain' no use for take it out in *malediction.* De nine shillin' is paid.
You scoop more fish—dat's the way.'

"So my fader he is go out early, early nex' mawny. He's scoop,
he's scoop. He's catch plenty fish before Old Man Savarin come.

" 'You ain't got 'nuff yet for fishin' on my land, eh? Come out of
dat,' Old Man Savarin is say.

" '*Saprie!* Ain't I pay nine shillin' for fish here?' my fader say.

" '*Oui*—you pay nine shillin' for fish here *wisout* my leave. But
you ain't pay nothin' for fish here *wis* my leave. You is goin' up before
de magistrate some more.'

"So he is fetch my fader up anoder time. An' de magistrate make
my fader pay twelve shillin' more!

" 'Well, I s'pose I can go fish on my fader's platform now,' my
fader is say.

"Old Man Savarin was laugh. 'Your honor, dis man tink he don't
have for pay me no rent, because you'll make him pay two fines for
trespass on my land.'

"So de magistrate told my fader he hain't got no more right for
go on his own platform than he was at the start. My fader is ver' angry.
He's cry, he's tear his shirt; but Old Man Savarin only say, 'I guess
I learn you one good lesson, Narcisse.'

"De whole village ain't told de old rascal how much dey was
angry 'bout dat, for Old Man Savarin is got dem all in debt at his big
store. He is grin, grin, and told everybody how he learn my fader two
good lesson. An' he is told my fader: 'You see what I'll be goin' for do
wis you if ever you go on my land again wisout you pay me rent.'

" 'How much you want?' my fader say.

" 'Half de fish you catch.'

" '*Monjee!* Never!'"

" 'Five dollar a year, den.'

" '*Saprie*, no. Dat's too much.'

" 'All right. Keep off my lan', if you hain't want anoder lesson.'

" 'You's a tief,' my fader say.

" 'Hermidas, make up Narcisse Laroque bill,' de old rascal say to his clerk. 'If he hain't pay that bill to-morrow, I sue him.'

"So my fader is scare mos' to death. Only my moder she's say, '*I'll* pay that bill, me.'

"So she's take the money she's saved up long time for make my weddin' when it come. An' she's paid de bill. So den my fader hain't scare no more, an' he is shake his fist good under Old Man Savarin's ugly nose. But dat old rascal only laugh an' say, 'Narcisse, you like to be fined some more, eh?'

" '*Tort Dieu.* You rob me of my place for fish, but I'll take my platform anyhow,' my fader is say.

" 'Yes, eh? All right— if you can get him wisout go on my land. But you go on my land, and see if I don't learn you anoder lesson,' Old Savarin is say.

"So my fader is rob of his platform, too. Nex'ting we hear, Frawce Seguin has rent dat platform for five dollars a year.

"Den de big fun begin. My fader an Frawce is cousin. All de time before den dey was good friend. But my fader he is go to Frawce Seguin's place an' he is told him, 'Frawce, I'll goin' lick you so hard you can't nev' scoop on my platform.'

"Frawce only laugh. Den Old Man Savarin come up de hill.

" 'Fetch him up to de magistrate an' learn him anoder lesson,' he is say to Frawce.

" 'What for?' Frawce say.

" 'For try to scare you.'

" 'He hain't hurt me none.'

" 'But he's say he will lick you.'

" 'Dat's only because he's vex,' Frawce say.

" '*Baptême! Non!* my fader say. 'I'll be goin' for lick you good, Frawce.'

" 'For sure?' Frawce say.

" '*Saprie!* Yes; for sure.'

" 'Well, dat's all right den, Narcisse. When you goin' for lick me?'

" 'First time I'll get drunk. I'll be goin' for get drunk dis same day.'

" 'All right, Narcisse. If you goin' get drunk for lick me, I'll be goin' get drunk for lick you'—*Canadien* hain't nev' fool 'nuff for fight, M'sieu, only if dey is got drunk.

"Well, my fader he's go on old Marceau's hotel, an' he's drink all day. Frawce Seguin he's go cross de road on Joe Maufraud's hotel, an' *he's* drink all day. When de night come, dey's bose stand out in front of de two hotel for fight.

"Dey's bose yell an' yell for make de oder feller scare bad before dey begin. Hermidas Laronde an' Jawnny Leroi dey's hold my fader for fear he's go 'cross de road for keel Frawce Seguin dead. Pierre Seguin an' Magloire Sauve is hold Frawce for fear he's come 'cross de road for keel my fader dead. And dose men fight dat way 'cross de road, till dey hain't hardly able for stand up no more.

"My fader he's tear his shirt and he's yell, 'Let me at him!' Frawce he's tear his shirt and he's yell, 'Let me at him!' But de men hain't goin' for let dem loose, for fear one is strike de oder ver' hard. De whole village is shiver 'bout dat offle fight—yes, seh, shiver bad!

"Well, dey's fight like dat for more as four hours, till dey hain't able for yell no more, an' dey hain't got no money left for buy wheeskey for de crowd. Den Marceau and Joe Maufraud tol' dem bose it was a shame for two cousins to fight so bad. An' my fader he's say he's ver' sorry dat he lick Frawce so hard, and dey's bose sorry. So dey's kiss one anoder good—only all their close is tore to pieces.

"An' what you tink 'bout Old Man Savarin? Old Man Savarin is just stand in front of his store all de time, an' he's say: 'I'll tink I'll fetch him *bose* hup to de magistrate, an' I'll learn him *bose* a lesson.'

"Me, I'll be only fifteen, but I hain't scare 'bout dat fight same like my moder is scare. No more is Alphonsine Seguin scare. She's seventeen, an' she wait for de fight to be all over. Den she take her fader home, same like I'll take my fader home for bed. Dat's after twelve o'clock of night.

"Nex' mawny early my fader he's groaned and he's groaned: 'Ah—ugh—I'm sick, sick, me. I'll be goin' for die dis time, for sure.'

" 'You get up an' scoop some fish,' my moder she's say, angry. 'Den you hain't be sick no more.'

" 'Ach—ugh—I'll hain't be able. Oh, I'll be so sick. An' I hain' got no place for scoop fish now no more. Frawce Sequin has rob my platform.'

" 'Take de nex' one lower down,' my moder she's say.

" 'Dat's Jawnny Leroi's.'

" 'All right for dat. Jawnny he's hire for run timber to-day.'

" 'Ugh—I'll not be able for get up. Send for M'sieu le Curé—I'll be goin' for die for sure.'

" '*Misère*, but dat's no *man!* Dat's a drunk pig,' my moder she's say, angry. 'Sick, eh? Lazy, lazy—dat's so. An' dere hain't no fish for de little chilluns, an' it's Friday mawny.' So my moder she's begin for cry.

"Well, M'sieu, I'll make de rest short; for de sun is all gone now. What you tink I do dat mawny? I take de big scoop-net an' I'll come up here for see if I'll be able for scoop some fish on Jawnny Leroi's platform. Only dere hain't nev' much fish dere.

"Pretty quick I'll look up and I'll see Alphonsine Seguin scoop, scoop on my fader's old platform. Alphonsine's fader is sick, sick, same like my fader, an' all de Seguin boys is too little for scoop, same like my brudders is too little. So dere Alphonsine she's scoop, scoop for breakfas'.

"What you tink I'll see some more? I'll see Old Man Savarin. He's watchin' from de corner of de cedar bush, an' I'll know ver' good what he's watch for. He's watch for catch my fader go on his own platform.

He's want for learn my fader anoder lesson. *Saprie!* dat's make me ver' angry, M'sieu!

"Alphonsine she's scoop, scoop plenty fish. I'll not be scoop none. Dat's make me more angry. I'll look up where Alponsine is, an' I'll talk to myself:—

" 'Dat's my fader's platform,' I'll be say. 'Dat's my fader's fish what you catch, Alphonsine. You hain't nev' be my cousin no more. It is mean, mean for Frawce Seguin to rent my fader's platform for please dat old rascal Savarin.' Mebby I'll not be so angry at Alphonsine, M'sieu, if I was able for catch some fish; but I hain't able—I don't catch none.

"Well, M'sieu, dat's de way for long time— half-hour mebby. Den I'll hear Alphonsine yell good. I'll look up de river some more. She's try for lift her net. She's try hard, hard, but she hain't able. De net is down in de rapid, an' she's only able for hang on to de hannle. Den I'll know she's got one big sturgeon, an' he's so big she can't pull him up.

"*Monjee!* what I care 'bout dat! I'll laugh me. Den I'll laugh good some more, for I'll want Alphonsine for see how I'll laugh big. And I'll talk to myself:—

" 'Dat's good for dose Seguins,' I'll say. 'De big sturgeon will pull away de net. Den Alphonsine she will lose her fader's scoop wis de sturgeon. Dat's good 'nuff for dose Seguins! Take my fader platform, eh?'

"For sure, I'll want for go an' help Alphonsine all de same—she's my cousin, an' I'll want for see de sturgeon, me. But I'll only just laugh, laugh. *Non, M'sieu;* dere was not one man out on any of de oder platform dat mawny for to help Alphonsine. Dey was all sleep ver' late, for dey was all out ver' late for see de offle fight I told you 'bout.

"Well, pretty quick, what you tink? I'll see Old Man Savarin goin' to my fader's platform. He's take hold for help Alphonsine, an' dey's bose pull, and pretty quick de big sturgeon is up on de platform. I'll be more angry as before.

"Oh, *tort Dieu!* What you tink come den? Why, dat Old Man Savarin is want for take de sturgeon!

"First dey hain't speak so I can hear, for de Rapid is too loud. But pretty quick dey's bose angry, and I hear dem talk.

" 'Dat's my fish,' Old Man Savarin is say. 'Didn't I save him? Wasn't you goin' for lose him, for sure?'

"Me—I'll laugh good. Dass *such* an old rascal.

" 'You get off dis platform, quick!' Alphonsine she's say.

" 'Give me my sturgeon,' he's say.

" 'Dat's a lie—it hain't your sturgeon. It's *my* sturgeon,' she's yell.

" 'I'll learn you one lesson 'bout dat,' he's say.

"Well, M'sieu, Alphonsine she's pull back de fish just when Old Man Savarin is make one grab. An' when she's pull back, she's step to one side, an' de old rascal he is grab at de fish, an' de heft of de sturgeon is make him fall on his face, so he's tumble in de Rapid when Alphonsine let go de sturgeon. So der's Old Man Savarin floating in de river—

and *me!* I'll don' care eef he's drown one bit!

"One time he is on his back, one time he is on his face, one time he is all under de water. For sure he's goin' for be draw into de *culbute* an' get drown' dead, if I'll not be able for scoop him when he's go by my platform. I'll want for laugh, but I'll be too much scare.

"Well, M'sieu, I'll pick up my fader's scoop and I'll stand out on de edge of de platform. De water is run so fast, I'm mos' 'fraid de old man is boun' for pull me in when I'll scoop him. But I'll not mind for dat, I'll throw de scoop an' catch him; an' for sure, he's hold on good.

"So dere's de old rascal in de scoop, but when I'll get him safe, I hain't able for pull him in one bit. I'll only be able for hold on an' laugh, laugh—he's look *ver'* queer! All I can do is to hold him dere so he can't go down de *culbute*. I'll can't pull him up if I'll want to.

"De old man is scare ver' bad. But pretty quick he's got hold of de cross-bar of de hoop, an' he's got his ugly old head up good.

" 'Pull me in,' he say, ver' angry.

" 'I'll hain't be able,' I'll say.

"Jus' den Alphonsine she's come 'long, an' she's laugh so she can't hardly hold on wis me to de hannle. I was laugh good some more. When de old villain see us have fun, he's yell: 'I'll learn you bose one lesson for this. Pull me ashore!'

" 'Oh! you's learn us bose one lesson, M'sieu Savarin, eh?' Alphonsine she's say. 'Well, den, us bose will learn M'sieu Savarin one lesson first. Pull him up a little,' she's say to me.

"So we pull him up, an' den Alphonsine she's say to me: 'Let out de hannle, quick'— and he's under de water some more. When we stop de net, he's got hees head up pretty quick.

" '*Monjee!* I'll be drown' if you don't pull me out,' he's mos' *cry.*

" 'Ver' well—if you's drown, your family be ver' glad,' Alphonsine she's say. 'Den they's got all your money for spend quick, quick.'

"M'sieu, dat scare him offle. He's begin for cry like one baby.

" 'Save me out,' he's say. 'I'll give you anything I've got.'

" 'How much?' Alphonsine she's say.

"He's tink, and he's say, 'Quarter dollar.'

"Alphonsine an' me is laugh, laugh.

" 'Save me,' he's cry some more. 'I hain't fit for die dis mawny.'

" 'You hain't fit for live no mawny,' Alphonsine she's say. 'One quarter dollar, eh? Where's my sturgeon?'

" 'He's got away when I fall in,' he's say.

" 'How much you goin' give me for lose my big sturgeon?' she's ask.

" 'How much you'll want, Alphonsine?'

" 'Two dollare.'

" 'Dat's too much for one sturgeon,' he's say. For all he was not feel fit for die, he was more 'fraid for pay out his money.

" 'Let him down some more,' Alphonsine she's say.

" 'Oh, misère, misère! I'll pay de two dollare,' he's say when his head come up some more.

" 'Ver' well, den,' Alphonsine she's say; 'I'll be willin' for save you, *me.* But you hain't scooped by *me.* You's in Marie's net. I'll only come for help Marie. You's her sturgeon'; an' Alphonsine she's laugh an' laugh.

" 'I didn't lost no sturgeon for Marie,' he's say.

" 'No, eh?' I'll say mysef. 'But you's steal my fader's platform. You's take his fishin' place. You's got him fined two times. You's make my moder pay his bill wis *my* weddin' money. What you goin' pay for all dat? You tink I'll be goin for mos' kill mysef pullin' you out for noting? When you ever do someting for anybody for noting, eh, M'sieu Savarin?'

" 'How much you want?' he's say.

" 'Ten dollare for de platform, dat's all.'

" 'Never—dat's robbery,' he's say, an' he's begin to cry like *ver'* li'll baby.

" 'Pull him hup, Marie, an' give him some more,' Alphonsine she's say.

" 'But de old rascal is so scare 'bout dat, dat he's say he's pay right off. So we's pull him up near to de platform, only we hain't big 'nuff fool for let him out of de net till he's take out his purse an' pay de twelve dollare.

"*Monjee*, M'sieu! If ever you see one angry old rascal! He not even stop for say: "T'ank you for save me from be drown' dead in the *culbute!* He's run for his house an' he's put on dry clo'es, and' he's go up to de magistrate first ting for learn me an' Alphonsine one big lesson.

" 'But de magistrate hain't ver' bad magistrate. He's only laugh an' he's say:—

" 'M'sieu Savarin, de whole river will be laugh at you for let two young girl take eet out of smart man like you like dat. Hain't you tink your life worth twelve dollare? Didn't dey save you from de *culbute? Monjee!* I'll tink de whole river not laugh so ver' bad if you pay dose young girl one hunder dollare for save you so kind.'

" 'One hunder dollare!' he's mos' cry. 'Hain't you goin' to learn dose girl one lesson for take advantage of me dat way?'

" 'Didn't you pay dose girl yoursef? Didn't you took out your purse yoursef? Yes, eh? Well, den, I'll goin' for learn you one lesson yourself, M'sieu Savarin,' de magistrate is say. 'Dose two young girl is ver' wicked, eh? Yes, dat's so. But for why? Hain't dey just do to you what you been doin' ever since you was in beesness? Don' I know? You hain' never yet got advantage of nobody wisout you rob him all you can, an' dose wicked young girl only act just like you give dem a lesson all your life.'

"An' de best fun was de whole river *did* laugh at M'sieu Savarin. An' my fader and Frawce Seguin is laugh most of all, till he's catch hup wis bose of dem anoder time. You come for see me some more, an' I'll tol' you 'bout dat."

McGrath's Bad Night

"Come, then, childer," said Mrs. McGrath, and took the big iron pot off. They crowded around her, nine of them, the eldest not more than thirteen, the youngest just big enough to hold out his yellow crockery bowl.

"The youngest first," remarked Mrs. McGrath, and ladled out a portion of the boiled cornmeal to each of the deplorable boys and girls. Before they reached the stools from which they had sprung up, or squatted again on the rough floor, they all burned their mouths in tasting the mush too eagerly. Then there they sat, blowing into their bowls, glaring into them, lifting their loaded iron spoons occasionally to taste cautiously, till the mush had somewhat cooled.

Then, *gobble-de-gobble-de-gobble*, it was all gone! Though they had neither sugar, nor milk, nor butter to it, they found it a remarkably excellent sample of mush, and wished only that, in quantity, it had been something more.

Peter McGrath sat close beside the cooking-stove, holding Number Ten, a girl-baby, who was asleep, and rocking Number Eleven, who was trying to wake up, in the low, unpainted cradle. He never took his eyes off Number Eleven; he could not bear to look around and see the nine devouring the cornmeal so hungrily. Perhaps McGrath could not, and certainly he would not,—he was so obstinate,—have told why he felt so reproached by the scene. He had felt very guilty for many weeks.

Twenty, yes, a hundred times a day he looked in a dazed way at his big hands, and they reproached him, too, that they had no work.

"Where is our smooth, broad-axe handle?" asked the fingers, "and why do not the wide chips fly?"

He was ashamed, too, every time he rose up, so tall and strong, with nothing to do, and eleven children and his wife next door to starvation; but if he had been asked to describe his feelings, he would merely have growled out angrily something against old John Pontiac.

"You'll take your sup now, Peter?" asked Mrs. McGrath, offering him the biggest of the yellow bowls. He looked up then, first at her forlorn face, then at the pot. Number Nine was diligently scraping off some streaks of mush that had run down the outside; Numbers Eight, Seven, Six, and Five were looking respectfully into the pot; Numbers Four, Three, Two, and One were watching the pot, the steaming bowl, and their father at the same time. Peter McGrath was very hungry.

"Yourself had better eat, Mary Ann," he said. "I'll be having mine after it's cooler."

Mrs. McGrath dipped more than a third of the bowlful back into the pot, and ate the rest with much satisfaction. The numerals watched her anxiously but resignedly.

"Sure it'll be cold entirely, Peter dear," she said, "and the warmth is so comforting. Give me little Norah now, the darlint! and be after eating your supper."

She had ladled out the last spoonful of mush, and the pot was being scraped inside earnestly by Nine, Eight, Seven, and Six. Peter took the bowl, and looked at his children.

The earlier numbers were observing him with peculiar sympathy, putting themselves in his place, as it were,· possessing the bowl in imagination; the others now moved their spoons absent-mindedly around in the pot, brought them empty to their mouths, mechanically, now and again, sucked them more or less, and still stared steadily at their father.

His inner walls felt glued together, yet indescribably hollow; the smell of the mush went up into his nostrils, and pungently provoked his palate and throat. He was famishing.

"Troth, then Mary Ann," he said, "there's no hunger in me to-night. Sure, I wish the childer wouldn't leave me the trouble of eating it. Come, then all of ye!"

The nine came promptly to his call. There were just twenty-two large spoonfuls in the bowl; each child received two; the remaining four went to the four youngest. Then the bowl was skilfully scraped by Number Nine, after which Number Seven took it, whirled a cup of water artfully round its interior, and with this put a fine finish on his meal.

Peter McGrath then searched thoughtfully in his trousers pockets, turning their corners up, getting pinches of tobacco dust out of their remotest recesses; he put his blouse pocket through a similar process. He found no pockets in his well-patched overcoat when he took it down, but he pursued the dust into its lining, and separated it carefully from little dabs of wool. Then he put the collection into an extremely old black clay pipe, lifted a coal in with his fingers, and took his supper.

It would be absurd to assert that, on this continent, a strong man could be so poor as Peter, unless he had done something very wrong or very foolish. Peter McGrath was, in truth, out of work because he had committed an outrage on economics. He had been guilty of the enormous error of misunderstanding, and trying to set at naught in his own person, the immutable law of supply and demand.

Fancying that a first-class hewer in a timber shanty had an inalienable right to receive at least thirty dollars a month, when the demand was only strong enough to yield him twenty-two dollars a month, Peter had refused to engage at the beginning of the winter.

"Now, Mr. McGrath, you're making a mistake," said his usual employer, old John Pontiac. "I'm offering you the best wages going, mind that. There's mighty little squared timber coming out this winter."

"I'm ready and willing to work, boss, but I'm fit to arn thirty dollars, surely."

"So you are, so you are, in good times, neighbor, and I'd be glad if men's wages were forty. That could only be with trade active, and a fine season for all of us; but I couldn't take out a raft this winter, and pay what you ask."

"I'd work extra hard. I'm not afeard of work."

"Not you, Peter. There never was a lazy bone in your body. Don't I know that well? But look, now: if I was to pay you thirty, I should have to pay all the other hewers thirty; and that's not all. Scorers and teamsters and road-cutters are used to getting wages in proportion to hewers. Why, it would cost me a thousand dollars a month to give you thirty! Go along, now, that's a good fellow, and tell your wife that you've hired with me."

But Peter did not go back. "I'm bound to have my rights, so I am," he said sulkily to Mary Ann when he reached the cabin. "The old boss is getting too hard like, and set on money. Twenty-two dollars! No! I'll go in to Stambrook and hire."

Mary Ann knew that she might as well try to convince a saw-log that its proper course was up-stream, as to protest against Peter's obstinacy. Moreover, she did think the offered wages very low, and had some hope he might better himself; but when he came back from Stambrook, she saw trouble ahead. He did not tell her that there, where his merits were not known, he had been offered only twenty dollars, but she surmised his disappointment.

"You'd better be after seeing the boss again, maybe, Peter dear," she said timidly.

"Not a step," he answered. "The boss'll be after me in a few days, you'll see." But there he was mistaken, for all the gangs were full.

After that Peter McGrath tramped far and wide, to many a backwoods hamlet, looking vainly for a job at any wages. The season was the worst ever known on the river, and before January the shanties were discharging men, so threatening was the outlook for lumbermen, and so glutted with timber the markets of the world.

Peter's conscience accused him every hour, but he was too stubborn to go back to John Pontiac. Indeed, he soon got it into his stupid head that the old boss was responsible for his misfortunes, and he consequently came to hate Mr. Pontiac very bitterly.

After supping on his pipeful of tobacco dust, Peter sat, straight-backed, leaning elbows on knees and chin on hands, wondering what on earth was to become of them all next day. For a man out of work there was not a dollar of credit at the little village store; and work! why, there was only one kind of work at which money could be earned in that district in the winter.

When his wife took Number Eleven's cradle into the other room, she heard him, through the thin partition of upright boards, pasted over with newspapers, moving round in the dim red flickering fire-light from the stove-grating.

The children were all asleep, or pretending it; Number Ten in the big straw bed, where she lay always between her parents; Number Eleven in her cradle beside; Nine crosswise at the foot; Eight, Seven, Six, Five, and Four in the other bed; One, Two, and Three curled up, without taking off their miserable garments, on the "locks" of straw beside the kitchen stove.

Mary Ann knew very well what Peter was moving round for.

She heard him groan, so low that he did not know he groaned, when he lifted off the cover of the meal barrel, and could feel nothing whatever therein. She had actually beaten the meal out of the cracks to make that last pot of mush. He knew that all the fish he had salted down in the summer were gone, that the flour was all out, that the last morsel of the pig had been eaten up long ago; but he went to each of the barrels as though he could not realize that there was really nothing left. There were four of those low groans.

"O God, help him! do help him! please do!" she kept saying to herself. Somehow, all her sufferings and the children's were light to her, in comparison, as she listened to that big, taciturn man groan, and him sore with the hunger.

When at last she came out, Peter was not there. He had gone out silently, so silently that she wondered, and was scared. She opened the door very softly, and there he was, leaning on the rail fence between their little rocky plot and the great river. She closed the door softly, and sat down.

There was a wide steaming space in the river, where the current ran too swiftly for any ice to form. Peter gazed on it for a long while. The mist had a friendly look; he was soon reminded of the steam from an immense bowl of mush! It vexed him. He looked up at the moon. The moon was certainly mocking him; dashing through light clouds, then jumping into a wide, clear space, where it soon became motionless, and mocked him steadily.

He had never known old John Pontiac to jeer any one, but there was his face in that moon,—Peter made it out quite clearly. He looked up the road to where he could see, on the hill half a mile distant, the shimmer of John Pontiac's big tin-roofed house. He thought he could make out the outlines of all the buildings,—he knew them so well,— the big barn, the stable, the smoke-house, the store-house for shanty supplies.

Pork barrels, flour barrels, herring kegs, syrup kegs, sides of frozen beef, hams and flitches of bacon in the smoke-house, bags of beans, chests of tea,—he had a vision of them all! Teamsters going off to the woods daily with provisions, the supply apparently inexhaustible.

And John Pontiac had refused to pay him fair wages!

Peter in exasperation shook his big fist at the moon; it mocked him worse than ever. Then out went his gaze to the space of mist; it was still more painfully like mush steam. His pigsty was empty, except of snow; it made him think again of the empty barrels in the cabin.

The children empty too, or would be tomorrow,—as empty as he felt that minute. How dumbly the elder ones would reproach him! and what would comfort the younger ones crying with hunger?

Peter looked again up the hill, through the walls of the store-house. He was dreadfully hungry.

"John! John!" Mrs. Pontiac jogged her husband. "John, wake up! there's somebody trying to get into the smoke-house."

"Eh—ugh—ah! I'm 'sleep—ugh." He relapsed again.

"John! John! wake up! There *is* somebody!"

"What—ugh—eh—what you say?"

"There's somebody getting into the smokehouse."

"Well, there's not much there."

"There's ever so much bacon and ham. Then there's the store-house open."

"Oh, I guess there's nobody."

"But there is, I'm sure. You must get up!"

They both got up and looked out of the window. The snow-drifts, the paths through them, the storehouse, the smoke-house, and the other white-washed out-buildings could be seen as clearly as in broad day. The smoke-house door was open!

Old John Pontiac was one of the kindest souls that ever inhabited a body, but this was a little too much. Still he was sorry for the man, no matter who, in that smoke-house,—some Indian probably. He must be caught and dealt with firmly; but he did not want the man to be too much hurt.

He put on his clothes and sallied forth. He reached the smoke-house; there was no one in it; there was a gap, though, where two long flitches of bacon *had* been!

John Pontiac's wife saw him go over to the store-house, the door of which was open too. He looked in, then stopped, and started back as if in horror. Two flitches tied together with a rope were on the floor, and inside was a man filling a bag with flour from a barrel.

"Well, well! this is a terrible thing," said old John Pontiac to himself, shrinking around a corner. "Peter McGrath! Oh, my! oh, my!"

He became hot all over, as if he had done something disgraceful himself. There was nobody that he respected more than that pigheaded Peter. What to do? He must punish him of course; but how? Jail?— for him with eleven children! "Oh, my! oh, my!" Old John wished he had not been awakened to see this terrible downfall.

"It will never do to let him go off with it," he said to himself after a little reflection. "I'll put him so that he'll know better another time."

Peter McGrath, as he entered the store-house, had felt that bacon heavier than the heaviest end of the biggest stick of timber he had ever helped to cant. He felt guilty, sneaking, disgraced; he felt that the literal Devil had first tempted him near the house, then all suddenly— with his own hunger pangs and thoughts of his starving family—swept him into the smoke-house to steal. But he had consented to do it; he had said he would take flour too,—and he would, he was so obstinate! And withal, he hated old John Pontiac worse than ever; for now he accused him of being the cause of his coming to this.

Then all of a sudden he met the face of Pontiac looking in at the door.

Peter sprang back; he saw Stambrook jail—he saw his eleven children and his wife—he felt himself a detected felon, and that was worst of all.

"Well, Peter, you'd ought to have come right in," were the words that came to his ears, in John Pontiac's heartiest voice. "The missis would have been glad to see you. We did go to bed a bit early, but there wouldn't have been any harm in an old neighbor like you waking us up. Not a word of that—hold on! listen to me. It would be a pity if old friends like you and me, Peter, couldn't help one another to a trifling loan of provisions without making a fuss over it." And old John, taking up the scoop, went on filling the bag as if that were a matter of course.

Peter did not speak; he could not.

"I was going round to your place to-morrow," resumed John, cheerfully, "to see if I couldn't hire you again. There's a job of hewing for you in the Conlonge shanty,— man gone off sick. But I can't give more'n twenty-two, or say twenty-three, seeing you're an old neighbor. What do you say?"

Peter still said nothing; he was choking.

"You had better have a bit of something more than bacon and flour, Peter," he went on, "and I'll give you a hand to carry the truck home. I guess your wife won't mind seeing me with you; then she'll know that you've taken a job with me again, you see. Come along and give me a hand to hitch the mare up. I'll drive you down."

"Ah—ah—Boss—Boss!" spoke Peter then, with terrible gasps between. "Boss—O, my God, Mr. Pontiac—I can't never look you in the face again!"

"Peter McGrath—old neighbor,"—and John Pontiac laid his hand on the shaking shoulder,—"I guess I know all about it; I guess I do. Sometimes a man is driven he don't know how. Now we will say no more about it. I'll load up, and you come right along with me. And mind, I'll do the talking to your wife."

Mary Ann McGrath was in a terrible frame of mind. What had become of Peter?

She had gone out to look down the road, and had been recalled by Number Eleven's crying. Number Ten then chimed in; Nine, too, awoke, and determined to resume his privileges as an infant. One after another they got up and huddled around her—craving, craving,—all but the three eldest, who had been well practised in the stoical philosophy by the gradual decrease of their rations. But these bounced up suddenly at the sound of a grand jangle of bells.

Could it be? Mr. Pontiac they had no doubt about; but was that real bacon that he laid on the kitchen table? Then a side of beef, a can of tea; next a bag of flour, and again an actual keg of sirup. Why, this was almost incredible! And, last, he came in with an immense round loaf of bread! The children gathered about it; old John almost sickened with sorrow for them, and hurrying out his jackknife, passed big hunks around.

"Well, now, Mrs. McGrath," he said during these operations, "I don't hardly take it kindly of you and Peter not to have come up to an old neighbor's house before this for a bit of a loan. It's well I met Peter to-night. Maybe he'd never have told me your troubles—not but what I blame myself for not suspecting how it was a bit sooner. I just made him take a little loan for the present. No, no; don't be talking like that! Charity! tut! tut! it's just an advance of wages. I've got a job for Peter; he'll be on pay to-morrow again."

At that Mary Ann burst out crying again. "Oh, God bless you, Mr. Pontiac! it's a kind man you are! May the saints be about your bed!"

With that she ran out to Peter, who still stood by the sleigh; she put the baby in his arms, and clinging to her husband's shoulder, cried more and more.

And what did obstinate Peter McGrath do? Why, he cried, too, with gasps and groans that seemed almost to kill him.

"Go in," he said; "go in, Mary Ann—go in—and kiss—the feet of him. Yes—and the boards—he stands on. You don't know what he's done—for me. It's broke I am—the bad heart of me—broke entirely—with the goodness of him. May the heavens be his bed!"

"Now, Mrs. McGrath," cried old John, "never you mind Peter; he's a bit light-headed to-night. Come away in and get a bite for him. I'd like a dish of tea myself before I go home." Didn't that touch on her Irish hospitality bring her in quickly!

"Mind you this, Peter," said the old man, going out then, "don't you be troubling your wife with any little secrets about to-night; that's between you and me. That's all I ask of you."

Thus it comes about that to this day, when Peter McGrath's fifteen children have helped him to become a very prosperous farmer, his wife does not quite understand the depth of worship with which he speaks of old John Pontiac.

Mrs. Pontiac never knew the story of the night.

"Never mind who it was, Jane," John said, turning out the light, on returning to bed, "except this,—it was a neighbor in sore trouble."

"Stealing—and you helped him! Well, John, such a man as you are!"

"Jane, I don't ever rightly know what kind of a man I might be, suppose hunger was cruel on me, and on you, and all of us! Let us bless God that he's saved us from the terriblest temptations, and thank him most especially when he inclines our hearts—inclines our hearts—that's all."

Privilege of the Limits

"Yes, indeed, my grandfather wass once in jail," said old Mrs. McTavish, of the county of Glengarry, in Ontario, Canada; "but that wass for debt, and he wass a ferry honest man whateffer, and he would not broke his promise—no, not for all the money in Canada. If you will listen to me, I will tell chust exactly the true story about that debt, to show you what an honest man my grandfather wass.

"One time Tougal Stewart, him that wass the poy's grandfather that keeps the same store in Cornwall to this day, sold a plough to my grandfather, and my grandfather said he would pay half the plough in October, and the other half whateffer time he felt able to pay the money. Yes, indeed, that was the very promise my grandfather gave.

"So he was at Tougal Stewart's store on the first of October early in the morning pefore the shutters wass taken off, and he paid half chust exactly to keep his word. Then the crop wass ferry pad next year, and the year after that one of his horses wass killed py lightning, and the next year his brother, that wass not rich and had a big family, died, and do you think wass my grandfather to let the family be disgraced without a good funeral? No, indeed. So my grandfather paid for the funeral, and there was at it plenty of meat and drink for eferypody, as wass the right Hielan' custom those days; and after the funeral my grandfather did not feel chust exactly able to pay the other half for the plough that year either.

"So, then, Tougal Stewart met my grandfather in Cornwall next day after the funeral, and asked him if he had some money to spare.

" 'Wass you in need of help, Mr. Stewart?' says my grandfather kindly. For if it's in any want you are Tougal,' says my grandfather, 'I will sell the coat off my back, if there is no other way to lend you a loan'; for that wass always the way of my grandfather with all his friends, and a bigger-hearted man there never wass in all Glengarry, or in Stormont, or in Dundas, moreofer.

" 'In want!' says Tougal—'in want, Mr. McTavish!' says he, very high. 'Would you wish to insult a gentleman, and him of the name of Stewart, that's the name of princes of the world?' he said, so he did.

"Seeing Tougal had his temper up, my grandfather spoke softly, being a quiet, peaceable man, and in wonder what he had said to offend Tougal.

" 'Mr. Stewart,' says my grandfather, 'it wass not in my mind to anger you whatefer. Only I thought, from your asking me if I had some money, that you might be looking for a wee bit of a loan, as many a gentleman has to do at times, an no shame to him at all,' said my grandfather.

" 'A loan?' says Tougal, sneering. 'A loan, is it? Where's your memory, Mr. McTavish? Are you not owing me half the price of the plough you've had these three years?'

" 'And wass you asking me for money for the other half of the plough?' says my grandfather, very astonished.

" 'Just that,' says Tougal.

" 'Have you no shame or honor in you?' says my grandfather, firing up. 'How could I feel able to pay that now, and me chust yesterday been giving my poor brother a funeral fit for the McTavishes' own grand-nephew, that wass as good chentleman's plood as any Stewart in Glengarry. You saw the expense I wass at, for there you wass, and I thank you for the politeness of coming, Mr. Stewart,' says my grandfather, ending mild, for the anger would never stay in him more than a minute, so kind was the nature he had.

" 'If you can spend money on a funeral like that, you can pay me for my plough,' says Stewart; for with buying and selling he wass become a poor creature, and the heart of a Hielan'man wass half gone out of him, for all he wass so proud of his name of monarchs and kings.

"My grandfather had a mind to strike him down on the spot, so he often said; but he thought of the time when he hit Hamish Cochrane in anger, and he minded the penances the priest put on him for breaking the silly man's jaw with that blow, so he smothered the heat that wass in him, and turned away in scorn. With that Tougal Stewart went to court, and sued my grandfather, puir mean creature.

"You might think that Judge Jones—him that wass judge in Cornwall before Judge Jarvis that's dead—would do justice. But no, he made it the law that my grandfather must pay at once, though Tougal Stewart could not deny what the bargain wass.

" 'Your Honor,' says my grandfather,'I said I'd pay when I felt able. And do I feel able now? No, I do not,' says he. It's a disgrace to Tougal Stewart to ask me, and himself telling you what the bargain wass,' said my grandfather. But Judge Jones said that he must pay, for all that he did not feel able.

" 'I will nefer pay one copper till I feel able,' says my grandfather; 'but I'll keep my Hielan' promise to my dying day, as I always done,' says he.

"And with that the old judge laughed, and said he would have to give judgment. And so he did; and after that Tougal Stewart got out an execution. But not the worth of a handful of oatmeal could the bailiff lay hands on, because my grandfather had chust exactly taken the precaution to give a bill of sale on his gear to his neighbor, Alexander Frazer, that could be trusted to do what was right after the law play was over.

"The whole settlement had great contempt for Tougal Stewart's conduct; but he wass a headstrong body, and once he begun to do wrong against my grandfather, he held on, for all that his trade fell away; and finally he had my grandfather arrested for debt, though you'll understand, sir, that he was owing Stewart nothing that he ought to pay when he didn't feel able.

"In those times prisoners for debt wass taken to jail in Cornwall, and if they had friends to give bail that they would not go beyond the posts that wass around the sixteen acres nearest the jail walls, the prisoners could go where they liked on that ground. This was called 'the privilege of the limits.' The limits, you'll understand, was marked by cedar posts painted white about the size of hitching-posts.

"The whole settlement wass ready to go bail for my grandfather if he wanted it, and for the health of him he needed to be in the open air, and so he gave Tuncan Macdonnell of the Greenfields, and Æneas Macdonald of the Sandfields, for his bail, and he promised, on his Hielan' word of honor, not to go beyond the posts. With that he went where he pleased, only taking care that he never put even the toe of his foot beyond a post, for all that some prisoners of the limits would chump ofer them and back again, or maybe swing round them, holding by their hands.

"Efery day the neighbors would go into Cornwall to give my grandfather the good word, and they would offer to pay Tougal Stewart for the other half of the plough, only that vexed my grandfather, for he wass too proud to borrow, and, of course, every day he felt less and less able to pay on account of him having to hire a man to be doing the spring ploughing and seeding and making the kale-yard.

"All this time, you'll mind, Tougal Stewart had to pay five shillings a week for my grandfather's keep, the law being so that if the debtor swore he had not five pounds' worth of property to his name, then the creditor had to pay the five shillings, and, of course, my grandfather had nothing to his name after he gave the bill of sale to Alexander Frazer. A great diversion it was to my grandfather to be reckoning up that if he lived as long as his father, that was hale and strong at ninety-six, Tougal would need to pay five or six hundred pounds for him, and there was only two pound five shillings to be paid on the plough.

"So it was like that all summer, my grandfather keeping heartsome, with the neighbors coming in so steady to bring him the news of the settlement. There he would sit, just inside one of the posts, for to pass his jokes, and tell what he wished the family to be doing next. This way it might have kept going on for forty years, only it came about that my grandfather's youngest child—him that was my father—fell sick, and seemed like to die.

"Well, when my grandfather heard that bad news, he wass in a terrible way, to be sure, for he would be longing to hold the child in his arms, so that his heart was sore and like to break. Eat he could not, sleep he could not: all night he would be groaning, and all day he would be walking around by the posts, wishing that he had not passed his Hielan' word of honor not to go beyond a post; for he thought how he could have broken out like a chentleman, and gone to see his sick child, if he had stayed inside the jail wall. So it went on three days and three nights pefore the wise thought came into my grandfather's head to show him how he need not go beyond the posts to see his little sick poy. With that he went straight to one of the white cedar posts, and pulled it up out of the hole, and started for home, taking great care to carry it in his hands pefore him, so he would not be beyond it one bit.

"My grandfather wass not half a mile out of Cornwall, which was only a little place in those days, when two of the turnkeys came after him.

" 'Stop, Mr. McTavish,' says the turnkeys.

" 'What for would I stop?' says my grandfather.

" 'You have broke your bail,' says they.

" 'It's a lie for you,' says my grandfather, for his temper flared up for anybody to say he would broke his bail. 'Am I beyond the post?' says my grandfather.

"With that they run in on him, only that he knocked the two of them over with the post, and went on rejoicing, like an honest man should, at keeping his word and overcoming them that would slander his good name. The only thing pesides thoughts of the child that troubled him was questioning whether he had been strictly right in turning round for to use the post to defend himself in such a way that it was nearer the jail than what he wass. But when he remembered how the jailer never complained of prisoners of the limits chumping ofer the posts, if so they chumped back again in a moment, the trouble went out of his mind.

"Pretty soon after that he met Tuncan Macdonnell of the Green-fields, coming into Cornwall with the wagon.

" 'And how is this, Glengatchie?' says Tuncan. 'For you were never the man to broke your bail.'

"Glengatchie, you'll understand, sir, is the name of my grand-father's farm.

" 'Never fear, Greenfields,' says my grandfather, 'for I'm not beyond the post.'

"So Greenfields looked at the post, and he looked at my grandfather, and he scratched his head a wee, and he seen it was so; and then he fell into a great admiration entirely.

" 'Get in with me, Glengatchie—it's proud I'll be to carry you home'; and he turned his team around. My grandfather did so, taking great care to keep the post in front of him all the time; and that way he reached home. Out comes my grandmother running to embrace him; but she had to throw her arms around the post and my grandfather's neck at the same time, he was that strict to be within his promise. Pefore going ben the house, he went to the back end of the kale-yard which was farthest from the jail, and there he stuck the post; and then he went back to see his sick child, while all the neighbors that came round was glad to see what a wise thought the saints had put into his mind to save his bail and his promise.

"So there he stayed a week till my father got well. Of course the constables came after my grandfather, but the settlement would not let the creatures come within a mile of Glengatchie. You might think, sir, that my grandfather would have stayed with his wife and weans, seeing the post was all the time in the kale-yard, and him careful not to go beyond it; but he was putting the settlement to a great deal of trouble day and night to keep the constables off, and he was fearful that they might take the post away, if ever they got to Glengatchie, and give him the name of false, that no McTavish ever had. So Tuncan Greenfields and Æneas Sandfield drove my grandfather back to the jail, him with the post behind him in the wagon, so as he would be between it and the jail. Of course Tougal Stewart tried his best to have the bail declared forfeited; but old Judge Jones only lauged, and said my grandfather was a Hielan' gentleman, with a very nice sense of honor, and that was chust exactly the truth.

"How did my grandfather get free in the end? Oh, then, that was because of Tougal Stewart being careless—him that thought he knew so much of the law. The law was, you will mind, that Tougal had to pay five shillings a week for keeping my grandfather in the limits. The money wass to be paid efery Monday, and it wass to be paid in lawful money of Canada, too. Well, would you belief that Tougal paid in four shillings in silver one Monday, and one shilling in coppers, for he took up the collection in church the day pefore, and it wass not till Tougal had gone away that the jailer saw that one of the coppers was a Brock copper,—a medal, you will understand, made at General Brock's death, and not lawful money of Canada at all. With that the jailer came out to my grandfather.

" 'Mr. McTavish,' says he, taking off his hat, 'you are a free man, and I'm glad of it.' Then he told him what Tougal had done.

" 'I hope you will not have any hard feelings toward me, Mr. McTavish,' said the jailer; and a decent man he wass, for all that there wass not a drop of Hielan' blood in him. 'I hope you will not think hard of me for not being hospitable to you, sir,' says he; 'but it's against the rules and regulations for the jailer to be offering the best he can command to the prisoners. Now that you are free, Mr. McTavish,' says the jailer, 'I would be a proud man if Mr. McTavish of Glengatchie would do me the honor of taking supper with me this night. I will be asking your leave to invite some of the gentlemen of the place, if you will say the word, Mr. McTavish,' says he.

"Well, my grandfather could never bear malice, the kind man he was, and he seen how bad the jailer felt, so he consented, and a great company came in, to be sure, to celebrate the occasion.

"Did my grandfather pay the balance on the plough? What for should you suspicion, sir, that my grandfather would refuse his honest debt? Of course he paid for the plough, for the crop was good that fall.

" 'I would be paying you the other half of the plough now, Mr. Stewart,' says my grandfather, coming in when the store was full.

" 'Hoich, but YOU are the honest McTavish!' says Tougal, sneering.

"But my grandfather made no answer to the creature, for he thought it would be unkind to mention how Tougal had paid out six pounds four shillings and eleven pence to keep him in on account of a debt of two pound five that never was due till it was paid."

Great Godfrey's Lament

"Hard to Angus! Man, his heart will be sore the night! In five years I have not heard him playing 'Great Godfrey's Lament,' " said old Alexander McTavish, as with him I was sitting of a June evening, at sundown, under a wide apple-tree of his orchard-lawn.

When the sweet song-sparrows of the Ottawa valley had ceased their plaintive strains, Angus McNeil began on his violin. This night, instead of "Tullochgorum" or "Roy's Wife" or "The March of the McNeils," or any merry strathspey, he crept into an unusual movement, and from a distance came the notes of an exceeding strange strain blent with the meditative murmur of the Rataplan Rapids.

I am not well enough acquainted with musical terms to tell the method of that composition in which the wail of a Highland coronach seemed mingled with such mournful crooning as I had heard often from Indian voyageurs north of Lake Superior. Perhaps that fancy sprang from my knowledge that Angus McNeil's father had been a younger son of the chief of the McNeil clan, and his mother a daughter of the greatest man of the Cree nation.

"Ay, but Angus is wae," sighed old McTavish. "What will he be seeing the now? It was the night before his wife died that he played yon last. Come, we will go up the road. He does be liking to see the people gather to listen."

We walked, maybe three hundred yards, and stood leaning against the ruined picket-fence that surrounds the great stone house built by Hector McNeil, the father of Angus, when he retired from his position as one of the "Big Bourgeois" of the famous Northwest Fur Trading Company.

The huge square structure of the four stories and a basement is divided, above the ground floor, into eight suites, some of four, and some of five rooms. In these suites the fur-trader, whose ideas were all patriarchal, had designed that he and his Indian wife, with his seven sons and their future families, should live to the end of his days and theirs. That was a dream at the time when his boys were all under nine years old, and Godfrey little more than a baby in arms.

The ground-floor is divided by a hall twenty-five feet wide into two long chambers, one intended to serve as a dining-hall for the multitude of descendants that Hector expected to see round his old age, the other as a withdrawing-room for himself and his wife, or for festive occasions. In this mansion Angus McNeil now dwelt alone.

He sat out that evening on a balcony at the rear of the hall, whence he could overlook the McTavish place and the hamlet that extends a quarter of a mile further down the Ottawa's north shore. His right side was toward the large group of French-Canadian people who had gathered to hear him play. Though he was sitting, I could make out that his was a gigantic figure.

"Ay—it will be just exactly 'Great Godfrey's Lament,' " McTavish whispered. "Weel do I mind him playing yon many's the night after Godfrey was laid in the mools. Then he played it no more till before his ain wife died. What is he seeing now? Man, it's weel kenned he has the second sight at times. Maybe he sees the pit digging for himself. He's the last of them."

"Who was Great Godfrey?" I asked, rather loudly.

Angus McNeil instantly cut short the "Lament," rose from his chair, and faced us.

"Aleck McTavish, who have you with you?" he called imperiously.

"My young cousin from the city, Mr. McNeil," said McTavish, with deference.

"Bring him in. I wish to spoke with you, Aleck McTavish. The young man that is not acquaint with the name of Great Godfrey McNeil can come with you. I will be at the great door."

"It's strange-like," said McTavish, as we went to the upper gate. "He has not asked me inside for near five years. I'm feared his wits is disordered, by his way of speaking. Mind what you say. Great Godfrey was most like a god to Angus."

When Angus McNeil met us at the front door I saw he was verily a giant. Indeed, he was a wee bit more than six and a half feet tall when he stood up straight. Now he was stooped a little, not with age, but with consumption,—the disease most fatal to men of mixed white and Indian blood. His face was dark brown, his features of the Indian cast, but his black hair had not the Indian lankness. It curled tightly round his grand head.

Without a word he beckoned us on into the vast withdrawing room. Without a word he seated himself beside a large oaken centre-table, and motioned us to sit opposite.

Before he broke silence, I saw that the windows of that great chamber were hung with faded red damask; that the heads of many a bull moose, buck, bear, and wolf grinned among guns and swords and claymores from its walls; that charred logs, fully fifteen feet long, remained in the fireplace from the last winter's burning; that there were three dim portraits in oil over the mantel; that the room contained much frayed furniture, once sumptuous of red velvet; and that many skins of wild beasts lay strewn over a hard-wood floor whose edges still retained their polish and faintly gleamed in rays from the red west.

That light was enough to show that two of the oil paintings must be those of Hector McNeil and his Indian wife. Between these hung one of a singularly handsome youth with yellow hair.

"Here my father lay dead," cried Angus McNeil, suddenly striking the table. He stared at us silently for many seconds, then again struck the table with the side of his clenched fist. "He lay here dead on this table—yes! It was Godfrey that straked him out all alone on this table. You mind Great Godfrey, Aleck McTavish."

"Well I do, Mr. McNeil; and your mother yonder,—a grand lady she was." McTavish spoke with curious humility, seeming wishful, I thought, to comfort McNeil's sorrow by exciting his pride.

"Ay—they'll tell hereafter that she was just exactly a squaw," cried the big man, angrily. "But grand she was, and a great lady, and a proud. Oh, man, man! but they were proud, my father and my Indian mother. And Godfrey was the pride of the hearts of them both. No wonder; but it was sore on the rest of us after they took him apart from our ways."

Aleck McTavish spoke not a word, and big Angus, after a long pause, went on as if almost unconscious of our presence:—

"White was Godfrey, and rosy of the cheek like my father; and the blue eyes of him would match the sky when you'll be seeing it up through a blazing maple on a clear day of October. Tall, and straight, and grand was Godfrey, my brother. What was the thing Godfrey could not do? The songs of him hushed the singing-birds on the tree, and the fiddle he would play to take the soul out of your body. There was not white one among us till he was born.

"The rest of us all were just Indians—ay, Indians, Aleck McTavish. Brown we were, and the desire of us was all for the woods and the river. Godfrey had white sense like my father, and often we saw the same look in his eyes. My God, but we feared our father!"

Angus paused to cough. After the fit he sat silent for some minutes. The voice of the great rapid seemed to fill the room. When he spoke again, he stared past our seat with fixed, dilated eyes, as if tranced by a vision.

"Godfrey, Godfrey—you hear! Godfrey, the six of us would go over the falls and not think twice of it, if it would please you, when you were little. Oich, the joy we had in the white skin of you, and the fine ways, till my father and mother saw we were just making an Indian of you, like ourselves! So they took you away; ay, and many's the day the six of us went to the woods and the river, missing you sore. It's then you began to look on us with that look that we could not see was different from the look we feared in the blue eyes of our father. Oh, but we feared him, Godfrey! And the time went by, and we feared and we hated you that seemed lifted up above your Indian brothers!"

"Oich, the masters they got to teach him!" said Angus, addressing himself again to my cousin. "In the Latin and the Greek they trained him. History books he read, and stories in song. Ay, and the manners of Godfrey! Well might the whole pride of my father and mother be on their one white son. A grand young gentleman was Godfrey,—Great Godfrey we called him, when he was eighteen.

"The fine, rich people that would come up in bateaux from Montreal to visit my father had the smile and the kind word for Godfrey; but they looked upon us with the eyes of the white man for the Indian. And that look we were more and more sure was growing harder in Godfrey's eyes. So we looked back at him with the eyes of the wolf that stares at the bull moose, and is fierce to pull him down, but dares not try, for the moose is too great and lordly.

"Mind you, Aleck McTavish, for all we hated Godfrey when we thought he would be looking at us like strange Indians—for all that, yet we were proud of him that he was our own brother. Well, we minded how he was all like one with us when he was little; and in the calm looks of him, and the white skin, and the yellow hair, and the grandeur of him, we had pride, do you understand? Ay, and in the strength of him we were glad. Would we not sit still and pleased when it was the talk how he could run quicker than the best, and jump higher than his head—ay, would we! Man, there was none could compare in strength with Great Godfrey, the youngest of us all!

"He and my father and mother more and more lived by themselves in this room. Yonder room across the hall was left to us six Indians. No manners, no learning had we; we were no fit company for Godfrey. My mother was like she was wilder with love of Godfrey the more he grew and the grander, and never a word for days and weeks together did she give to us. It was Godfrey this, and Godfrey that, and all her thought was Godfrey!

"Most of all we hated him when she was lying dead here on this table. We six in the other room could hear Godfrey and my father groan and sigh. We would step softly to the door and listen to them kissing her that was dead,—them white, and she Indian like ourselves, —and us not daring to go in for the fear of the eyes of our father. So the soreness was in our hearts so cruel hard that we would not go in till the last, for all their asking. My God, my God, Aleck McTavish, if you saw her! she seemed smiling like at Godfrey, and she looked like him then, for all she was brown as November oak-leaves, and he white that day as the froth on the rapid.

"That put us farther from Godfrey than before. And farther yet we were from him after, when he and my father would be walking up and down, up and down, arm in arm, up and down the lawn in the evenings. They would be talking about books, and the great McNeils in Scotland. The six of us knew we were McNeils, for all we were Indians, and we would listen to the talk of the great pride and the great deeds of the McNeils that was our own kin. We would be drinking the whiskey if we had it, and saying: 'Godfrey to be the only McNeil! Godfrey to take all the pride of the name of us!' Oh, man, man! but we hated Godfrey sore."

Big Angus paused long, and I seemed to see clearly the two fair-haired, tall men walking arm in arm on the lawn in the twilight, as if unconscious or careless of being watched and overheard by six sore-hearted kinsmen.

"You'll mind when my father was thrown from his horse and carried into this room, Aleck McTavish? Ay, well you do. But you nor no other living man but me knows what came about the night that he died.

"Godfrey was alone with him. The six of us were in yon room. Drink we had, but cautious we were with it, for there was a deed to be done that would need all our senses. We sat in a row on the floor— we were Indians—it was our wigwam—we sat on the floor to be against the ways of them two. Godfrey was in here across the hall from us; alone he was with our white father. He would be chief over us by the will, no doubt,—and if Godfrey lived through that night it would be strange.

"We were cautious with the whiskey, I told you before. Not a sound could we hear of Godfrey or of my father. Only the rapid, calling and calling,—I mind it well that night. Ay, and well I mind the striking of the great clock,—tick, tick, tick, tick, tick,—I listened and I dreamed on it till I doubted but it was the beating of my father's heart.

"Ten o'clock was gone by, and eleven was near. How many of us sat sleeping I know not; but I woke up with a start, and there was Great Godfrey, with a candle in his hand, looking down strange at us, and us looking up strange at him.

" 'He is dead,' Godfrey said.

"We said nothing.

" 'Father died two hours ago,' Godfrey said.

"We said nothing.

" 'Our father is white,—he is very white,' Godfrey said, and he trembled. 'Our mother was brown when she was dead.'

"Godfrey's voice was wild.

" 'Come, brothers, and see how white is our father,' Godfrey said.

"No one of us moved.

" 'Won't you come? In God's name, come,' said Godfrey. 'Oich—but it is very strange! I have looked in his face so long that now I do not know him for my father. He is like no kin to me, lying there. I am alone, alone.'

"Godfrey wailed in a manner. It made me ashamed to hear his voice like that—him that looked like my father that was always silent as a sword—him that was the true McNeil.

" 'You look at me, and your eyes are the eyes of my mother,' says Godfrey, staring wilder. 'What are you doing here, all so still? Drinking the whiskey? I am the same as you. I am your brother. I will sit with you, and if you drink the whiskey, I will drink the whiskey, too.'

"Aleck McTavish! with that he sat down on the floor in the dirt and litter beside Donald, that was oldest of us all.

" 'Give me the bottle,' he said. 'I am as much Indian as you, brothers. What you do I will do, as I did when I was little, long ago.'

"To see him sit down in his best,—all his learning and his grand manners as if forgotten,—man, it was like as if our father himself was turned Indian, and was low in the dirt!

"What was in the heart of Donald I don't know, but he lifted the bottle and smashed it down on the floor.

" 'God in heaven! what's to become of the McNeils! You that was the credit of the family, Godfrey!' says Donald with a groan.

"At that Great Godfrey jumped to his feet like he was come awake.

" 'You're fitter to be the head of the McNeils that I am, Donald,' says he; and with that the tears broke out of his eyes, and he cast himself into Donald's arms. Well, with that we all began to cry as if our hearts would break. I threw myself down on the floor at Godfrey's feet, and put my arms round his knees the same as I'd lift him up when he was little. There I cried, and we all cried around him, and after a bit I said:

" 'Brothers, this was what was in the mind of Godfrey. He was all alone in yonder. We are his brothers, and his heart warmed to us, and he said to himself, it was better to be like us than to be alone, and he thought if he came and sat down and drank the whiskey with us, he would be our brother again, and not be any more alone.'

" 'Ay, Angus, Angus, but how did you know that?' says Godfrey, crying; and he put his arms round my neck, and lifted me up till we were breast to breast. With that we all put our arms some way round one another and Godfrey, and there we stood sighing and swaying and sobbing a long time, and no man saying a word.

" 'Oh, man, Godfrey dear, but our father is gone, and who can talk with you now about the Latin, and the history books, and the great McNeils—and our mother that's gone? says Donald; and the thought of it was such pity that our hearts seemed like to break.

"But Godfrey said: 'We will talk together like brothers. If it shames you for me to be like you, then I will teach you all they taught me, and we will all be like our white father.'

"So we all agreed to have it so, if he would tell us what to do. After that we came in here with Godfrey, and we stood looking at my father's white face. Godfrey all alone had straked him out on this table, with the silverpieces on the eyes that we had feared. But the silver we did not fear. Maybe you will not understand it, Aleck McTavish, but our father never seemed such close kin to us as when we would look at him dead, and at Godfrey, that was the pricutre of him, living and kind.

"After that you know what happened yourself."

"Well I do, Mr. McNeil. It was Great Godfrey that was the father to you all," said my cousin.

"Just that, Aleck McTavish. All that he had was ours to use as we would,—his land, money, horses, this room, his learning. Some of us could learn one thing and some of us could learn another, and some could learn nothing, not even how to behave. What I could learn was the playing of the fiddle. Many's the hour Godfrey would play with me while the rest were all happy around.

"In great content we lived like brothers, and proud to see Godfrey as white and fine and grand as the best gentleman that ever came up to visit him out of Montreal. Ay, in great content we lived all together till the consumption came on Donald, and he was gone. Then it came and came back, and came back again, till Hector was gone, and Ranald was gone, and in ten years' time only Godfrey and I were left. Then both of us married, as you know. But our children died as fast as they were born, almost, for the curse seemed on us. Then his wife died, and Godfrey sighed and sighed ever after that.

"One night I was sleeping with the door of my room open, so I could hear if Godfrey needed my help. The cough was on him then. Out of a dream of him looking at my father's white face I woke and went to his bed. He was not there at all.

"My heart went cold with fear, for I heard the rapid very clear, like the nights they all died. Then I heard the music begin down stairs, here in this chamber where they were all laid out dead,—right here on this table where I will soon lie like the rest. I leave it to you to see it done, Aleck McTavish, for you are a Highlandman by blood. It was that I wanted to say to you when I called you in. I have seen himself in my coffin three nights. Nay, say nothing; you will see.

"Hearing the music that night, down I came softly. Here sat Godfrey, and the kindest look was on his face that ever I saw. He had his fiddle in his hand, and he played about all our lives.

"He played about how we all came down from the North in the big canoe with my father and mother, when we were little children and him a baby. He played of the rapids we passed over, and of the rustling of the poplar-trees and the purr of the pines. He played till the river you hear now was in the fiddle, with the sound of our paddles, and the fish jumping for flies. He played about the long winters when we were young, so that the snow of those winters seemed falling again. The ringing of our skates on the ice I could hear in the fiddle. He played through all our lives when we were young and going in the woods yonder together—and then it was the sore lament began!

"It was like as if he played how they kept him away from his brothers, and him at his books thinking of them in the woods, and him hearing the partridges' drumming, and the squirrels' chatter, and all the little birds singing and singing. Oich, man, but there's no words for the sadness of it!"

Old Angus ceased to speak as he took his violin from the table and struck into the middle of "Great Godfrey's Lament." As he played, his wide eyes looked past us, and the tears streamed down his brown cheeks. When the woful strain ended, he said, staring past us: "Ay Godfrey, you were always our brother."

Then he put his face down in his big brown hands, and we left him without another word.

Dour Davie's Drive

Pinnager was on snow-shoes, making a bee-line toward his field of sawlogs dark on the ice of Wolverine River. He crossed shanty roads, trod heaps of brush, forced his way through the tops of felled pines, jumped from little crags into seven feet of snow—Pinnager's men called him "a terror on snow-shoes." They never knew the direction from which he might come—an ignorance which kept them all busy with axe, saw, cant-hook, and horses over the two square miles of forest comprising his "cut."

It was "make or break" with Pinnager. He had contracted to put on the ice all the logs he might make; for every one left in the woods he must pay stumpage and forfeit. Now his axe-men had done such wonders that Pinnager's difficulty was to get his logs hauled out.

Teams were scarce that winter. The shanty was eighty miles from any settlement; ordinary teamsters were not eager to work for a small speculative jobber, who might or might not be able to pay in the spring. But Pinnager had some extraordinary teamsters, sons of farmers who neighbored him at home, and who were sure he would pay them, though he should have to mortgage his land.

The time was late February; seven feet of snow, crusted, on the level; a thaw might turn the whole forest floor to slush; but if the weather should "hold hard" for six weeks longer, Pinnager might make and not break. Yet the chances were heavily against him.

Any jobber so situated would feel vexed on hearing that one of his best teams had suddenly been taken out of his service. Pinnager, crossing a shanty road with the stride of a moose, was hailed by Jamie Stuart with the news:

"Hey, boss, hold on! Davie McAndrews' leg's broke. His load slewed at the side hill—log catched him against a tree."

"Where is he?" shouted Pinnager furiously.

"Carried him to the shanty."

"Where are his horses?"

"Stable."

"Tell Aleck Dunbar to go get them out. He must take Davie's place—confound the lad's carelessness!"

"Davie says no; won't let any other man drive his horses."

"He won't? I'll show him!" and Pinnager made a bee-line for his shanty. He was choking with rage, all the more so because he knew that nothing short of breaking Davie McAndrews' neck would break Davie McAndrews' stubbornness, a reflection that cooled Pinnager before he reached the shanty.

The cook was busy about the caboose fire, getting supper for fifty-three devourers, when Pinnager entered the low door, and made straight for one of the double tier of dingy bunks. There lay a youth of eighteen, with an unusual pallor on his weather-beaten face, and more than the usual sternness about his formidable jaw.

"What's all this, Davie? You sure the leg's broke? I'd 'a thought you old enough to take care."

"You would?" said Davie grimly. "And yourself not old enough to have yon piece of road mended—you that was so often told about it!"

"When you knew it was bad, the more you should take care."

"And that's true, Pinnager. But no use in you and me choppin' words. I'm needing a doctor's hands on me. Can you set a bone?"

"No, I'll not meddle with it. Maybe Jock Scott can; but I'll send you out home. A find loss I'll be at! Confound it—and me like to break for want of teams!"

"I've thocht o' yer case, Pinnager," said Davie, with a curious judicial air. "It's sore hard for ye; I ken that well. There's me and me feyther's horses gawn off, and you countin' on us. I feel for ye, so I do. But I'll no put you to ony loss in sendin' me out."

"Was you thinking to tough it through here, Davie? No, you'll not chance it. Anyway, the loss would be the same—more, too. Why, if I send out for the doctor, there's a team off for full five days, and the expense of the doctor! Then he mightn't come. Wow, no! it's out you must go."

"What else?" said Davie coolly. "Would I lie here till spring and my leg mendin' into the Lord kens what-like shape? Would I be lettin' ony ither drive the horses my feyther entrustit to my lone? Would I be dependin' on Mr. Pinnager for keep, and me idle? Man, I'd eat the horses' heads off that way; at home they'd be profit to my feyther. So it's me and them that starts at gray the morn's morn."

"Alone!" exclaimed Pinnager.

"Just that, man. What for no?"

"You're light-headed, Davie. A lad with his leg broke can't drive three days."

"Maybe yes and maybe no. I'm for it, onyhow."

"It may snow, it may——"

"Aye, or rain, or thaw, or hail; the Lord's no in the habit o' makin' weather suit ony but himsel'. But I'm gawn; the cost of a man wi' me would eat the wages ye're owing my feyther."

"I'll lose his team, anyhow," said Pinnager, "and me needing it bad. A driver with you could bring back the horses."

"Nay, my feyther will trust his beasts to nane but himsel' or his sons. But I'll have yer case in mind, Pinnager; it's a sore needcessity you're in. I'll ask my feyther to send back the team, and another to the tail of it; it's like that Tam and Neil will be home by now. And I'll spread word how ye're needin' teams, Pinnager; it's like your neighbors will send ye in sax or eight spans."

"Man, that's a grand notion, Davie! But you can't go alone; it's clean impossible."

"I'm gawn, Pinnager."

"You can't turn out in seven feet of snow when you meet loading.

You can't water or feed your horses. There's forty miles the second day, and never a stopping-place; your horses can't stand it."

"I'm wae for the beasts, Pinnager; but they'll have no force but to travel dry and hungry if that's set for them."

"You're bound to go?"

"Div you tak' me for an idjit to be talkin' and no meanin' it? Off wi' ye, man! The leg's no exactly a comfort when I'm talkin'."

"Why, Davie, it must be hurting you terrible!" Pinnager had almost forgotten the broken leg, such was Davie's composure.

"It's no exactly a comfort, I said. Get you gone, Pinnager; your men may be idlin'. Get you gone, and send in Jock Scott, if he's man enough to handle my leg. I'm wearyin' just now for my ain company."

As Davie had made his programme, so it stood. His will was inflexible to protests. Next morning at dawn they set him on a hay-bed in his low, unboxed sleigh. A bag of oats supported his back; his unhurt leg was braced against a piece of plank spiked down. Jock Scott had pulled the broken bones into what he thought their place, and tied the leg up in splints of cedar.

The sleigh was enclosed by stakes, four on each side, all tied together by stout rope. The stake at Davie's right hand was shortened, that he migh hang his reins there. His water-bucket was tied to another stake, and his bag of provisions to a third. He was warm in a coon-skin coat, and four pairs of blankets under or over him.

At the last moment Pinnager protested: "I must send a man to drive. It sha'n't cost you a cent, Davie."

"Thank you kindly, Pinnager," said Davie gravely. "I'll tell that to your credit at the settlement. But ye're needin' all your help, and I'd take shame to worsen your chances. My feyther's horses need no drivin' but my word."

Indeed, they would "gee," "haw," or "whoa" like oxen, and loved his voice. Round-barrelled, deep-breathed, hardy, sure-footed, active, gentle, enduring, brave, and used to the exigencies of "bush roads," they would take him through safely if horses' wit could.

Davie had uttered never a groan after those involuntary ones forced from him when the log, driving his leg against a tree, had made him almost unconscious. But the pain-sweat stood beaded on his face during the torture of carrying him to the sleigh. Not a sound from his lips, though! They could guess his sufferings from naught but his hard breathing through the nose, that horrible sweat, and the iron set of his jaw. After they had placed him, the duller agony that had kept him awake all night returned; he smiled grimly, and said, "That's a comfort."

He had eaten and drunk heartily; he seemed strong still; but what if his sleigh should turn over at some sidling place of the rude, lonely, and hilly forest road?

As Davie chirruped to his horses and was off, the men gave him a cheer; then Pinnager and all went away to labor fit for mighty men, and the swinging of axes and the crashing of huge pines and the tumbling of logs from rollways left them fancy-free to wonder how

Davie could ever brace himself to save his broken leg at the *cahots*.

The terrible *cahots*—plunges in snow-roads! But for them Davie would have suffered little more than in a shanty bunk. The track was mostly two smooth ruts separated by a ridge so high and hard that the sleigh-bottom often slid on it. Horses less sure-footed would have staggered much, and bitten crossly at one another while trotting in those deep, narrow ruts, but Davie's horses kept their "jog" amiably, tossing their heads with glee to be traveling toward home.

The clink of trace-chains, the clack of harness, the glide of runners on the hard, dry snow, the snorting of the frosty-nosed team, the long whirring of startled grouse—Davie heard only these sounds, and heard them dreamily in the long, smooth flights between *cahots*.

Overhead the pine tops were a dark canopy with little fields of clear blue seen through the rifts of green; on the forest floor small firs bent under rounding weights of snow which often slid off as if moved by the stir of partridge wings; the fine tracery of hemlocks stood clean; and birches snuggled in snow that mingled with their curling rags. Sometimes a breeze eddied downward in the aisles, and then all the undergrowth was a silent commotion of snow, shaken and falling. Davie's eyes noted all things unconsciously; in spite of his pain he felt the enchantment of the winter woods until—another *cahot!* he called his team to walk.

Never was one *cahot* without many in succession; he gripped his stake hard at each, braced his sound leg, and held on, feeling like to die with the horrible thrust of the broken one forward and then back; yet always his will ordered his desperate senses.

Eleven o'clock! Davie drew up before the half-breed Peter Whiteduck's midwood stopping-place, and briefly explained his situation.

"Give my horses a feed," he went on. "There's oats in this bag. I'll no be moved mysel'. Maybe you'll fetch me a tin of tea; I've got my own provisions." So he ate and drank in the zero weather.

"You'll took lil' drink of whiskey," said Peter, with commiseration, as Davie was starting away.

"I don't use it."

"You'll got for need some 'fore you'll see de Widow Green place. Dass twenty-tree mile."

"I will need it, then," said Davie, and was away.

Evening had closed in when the bunch of teamsters awaiting supper at Widow Green's rude inn heard sleigh-bells, and soon a shout outside:

"Come out, some one!"

That was an insolence in the teamsters' code. Come out, indeed! The Widow Green, bustling about with fried pork, felt outraged. To be called out!—of her own house!—like a dog!—not she!

"Come out here, somebody!" Davie shouted again.

"G'out and break his head one of you," said fighting Moses Frost. "To be shoutin' like a lord!" Moses was too great a personage to go out and wreak vengeance on an unknown.

Narcisse Larocque went—to thrash anybody would be glory for Narcisse, and he felt sure that Moses would not, in these circumstances, let anybody thrash him.

"What for you shout lak' dat? Call mans hout, hey?" said Narcisse. "I'll got good mind for broke your head, me!"

"Hi, there, men!" Davie ignored Narcisse as he saw figures through the open door. "Some white man come out. My leg's broke."

Oh, then the up-jumping of big men! Moses, striding forth, ruthlessly shoved Narcisse, who lay and cowered with legs up as a dog trying to placate an angry master. Then Moses carried Davie in as gently as if the young stalwart had been a girl baby, and laid him on the widow's one spare bed.

That night Davie slept soundly for four hours, and woke to consciousness that his leg was greatly swollen. He made no moan, but lay in the darkness listening to the heavy breathing of the teamsters on the floor. They could do nothing for him; why should he awaken them? As for pitying himself, Davie could do nothing so fruitless. He fell to plans for getting teams in to Pinnager, for this young Scot's practical mind was horrified at the thought that the man should fail financially when ten horses might give him a fine profit for his winter's work.

Davie was away at dawn, every slight jolt giving his swollen leg pain almost unendurable, as if edges of living bone were grinding together and also tearing cavities in the living flesh; but he must endure it, and well too, for the teamsters had warned him he must meet "strings of loadin' " this day.

The rule of the long one-tracked road into the wilderness is, of course, that empty outgoing sleighs shall turn out for incoming laden ones. Turn out into seven feet of snow! Davie trusted that incoming teamsters would handle his floundering horses, and he set his mind to plan how they might save him from tumbling about on his turned-out sleigh.

About nine o'clock, on a winding road, he called, "Whoa!" and his bays stood. A sleigh piled with baled hay confronted him thirty yards distant. Four others followed closely; the load drawn by the sixth team was hidden by the woodland curve. No teamsters were visible; they must be walking behind the procession; and Davie wasted no strength in shouting. On came the laden teams, till the steam of the leaders mingled with the clouds blown by his bays. At that halt angry teamsters, yelling, ran forward and sprang, one by one, up on their loads, the last to grasp reins being the leading driver.

"Turn out, you fool!" he shouted. Then to his comrades behind, "There's a blamed idyit don't know enough to turn out for loading!"

Davie said nothing. It was not till one angry man was at his horses' heads and two more about to tumble his sleigh aside that he spoke:

"My leg is broke."

"Gah! G'way! A man driving with his leg broke! You're lying! Come, get out and tramp down snow for your horses! It's your back ought to be broke—stoppin' loadin'!"

"My leg is broke," Davie calmly insisted.

"You mean it?"

Davie threw off his blankets.

"Begor, it is broke!" "And him drivin' himself!" "It's a terror!" "Great spunk entirely!" Then the teamsters began planning to clear the way.

That was soon settled by Davie's directions: "Tramp down the crust for my horses; onhitch them; lift my sleigh out on the crust; pass on; then set me back on the road."

Half an hour was consumed by the operation—thrice repeated before twelve o'clock. Fortunately Davie came on the last "string" of teams halted for lunch by the edge of a lake. The teamsters fed and watered his horses, gave him hot tea, and with great admiration saw him start for an afternoon drive of twenty-two miles.

"You'll not likely meet any teams," they said. "The last of the 'loading' that's like to come in soon is with ourselves."

How Davie got down the hills, up the hills, across the rivers and over the lakes of that terrible afternoon he could never rightly tell.

"I'm thinkin' I was light-heided," he said afterward. "The notion was in me somehow that the Lord was lookin' to me to save Pinnager's bits of children. I'd waken out of it at the *cahots*—there was mair than enough. On the smooth my head would be strange-like, and I mind but the hinder end of my horses till the moon was high and me stoppit by McGraw's."

During the night at McGraw's his head was cleared by some hours of sound sleep, and next morning he insisted on traveling, though snow was falling heavily.

"My feyther's place is no more than a bittock ayont twenty-eight miles," he said. "I'll make it by three of the clock, if the Lord's willin', and get the doctor's hands on me. It's my leg I'm thinkin' of savin'. And mind ye, McGraw, you've promised me to send in your team to Pinnager."

Perhaps people who have never risen out of bitter poverty will not understand Davie's keen anxiety about Pinnager and Pinnager's children; but the McAndrews and Pinnagers and all their neighbors of "the Scotch settlement" had won up by the tenacious labor and thrift of many years. Davie remembered well how, in his early boyhood, he had often craved more food and covering. Pinnager and his family should not be thrown back into the gulf of poverty if Davie McAndrews' will could save them.

This day his road lay through a country thinly settled, but he could see few cabins through the driving storm. The flagging horses trotted steadily, as if aware that the road would become worse the longer they were on it, but about ten o'clock they inclined to stop where Davie could dimly see a long house and a shed with a team and sleigh standing in it. Drunken yells told him this must be Black Donald Donaldson's notorious tavern; so he chirruped his horses onward.

Ten minutes later yells and sleigh-bells were following him at a furious pace. Davie turned head and shouted; still the drunken men shrieked and came on. He looked for a place to turn out—none! He dared not stop his horses lest the gallopers, now close behind him, should be over him and his low sleigh. Now his team broke into a run at the noises, but the fresh horses behind sped faster. The men were hidden from Davie by their crazed horses. He could not rise to appeal; he could not turn to daunt the horses with his whip; their front-hoofs, rising high, were soon within twenty feet of him. Did his horses slacken, the others would be on top of him, kicking and tumbling.

The *cahots* were numerous; his yells for a halt became so much like screams of agony that he took shame of them, shut his mouth firmly, and knew not what to do. Then suddenly his horses swerved into the cross-road to the Scotch settlement, while the drunkards galloped away on the main road, still lashing and yelling. Davie does not know to this day who the men were.

Five hours later David McAndrews, the elder, kept at home by the snowstorm, heard bells in his lane, and looked curiously out of the sitting-room window.

"Losh, Janet!" he said, most deliberately. "I wasna expeckin' Davie; here he's back wi' the bays."

He did not hurry out to meet his fourth son, for he is a man who hates the appearance of haste; but his wife did, and came rushing back through the kitchen.

"It's Davie himsel'! He's back wi' his leg broke! He's come a' the way by his lone!"

"Hoot-toot, woman! Ye're daft!"

"I'm no daft; come and see yoursel'. Wae's me, my Davie's like to die! Me daft, indeed! Ye'll need to send Neil straight awa' to the village for Doctor Aberdeen."

And so dour Davie's long drive was past. While his brother carried him in, his will was occupied with the torture, but he had scarcely been laid on his bed when he said, very respectfully—but faintly—to his father:

"You'll be sendin' Neil oot for the doctor, sir? Aye; then I'd be thanfu' if you'd give Aleck leave to tak' the grays and warn the settlement that Pinnager's needin' teams sorely. He's like to make or break; if he gets sax or eight spans in time he's a made man."

That was enough for the men of the Scotch settlement. Pinnager got all the help he needed; and yet he is far from as rich to-day as Davie McAndrews, the great Brazeau River lumberman, who walks a little lame of his left leg.

Red-Headed Windego

Big Baptiste Seguin, on snow-shoes nearly six feet long, strode mightily out of the forest, and gazed across the treeless valley ahead.

"Hooraw! No choppin' for two mile!" he shouted.

"Hooraw!" Bully! Hi-yi!" yelled the axemen, Pierre, "Jawnny," and "Frawce," two hundred yards behind. Their cries were taken up by the two chain-bearers still farther back.

"Is it a lake, Baptiste?" cried Tom Dunscombe, the young surveyor, as he hurried forward through balsams that edged the woods and concealed the open space from those among the trees.

"No, seh; only a beaver meddy."

"Clean?"

"Clean! Yesseh! Clean's your face. Hain't no tree for two mile if de line is go right."

"Good! We shall make seven miles to-day," said Tom, as he came forward with immense strides, carrying a compass and Jacob's-staff. Behind him the axemen slashed along, striking white slivers from the pink and scaly columns of red pines that shot up a hundred and twenty feet without a branch. If any underbrush grew there, it was beneath the eight-feet-deep February snow, so that one could see far away down a multitude of vaulted, converging aisles.

Our young surveyor took no thought of the beauty and majesty of the forest he was leaving. His thoughts and those of his men were set solely on getting ahead; for all hands had been promised double pay for their whole winter, in case they succeeded in running a line round the disputed Moose Lake timber berth before the tenth of April.

Their success would secure the claim of their employer, Old Dan McEachran, whereas their failure would submit him perhaps to the loss of the limit, and certainly to a costly lawsuit with Old Rory Carmichael, another potentate of the Upper Ottawa.

At least six weeks more of fair snow-shoeing would be needed to "blaze" out the limit, even if the unknown country before them should turn out to be less broken by cedar swamps and high precipices than they feared. A few days' thaw with rain would make slush of the eight feet of snow, and compel the party either to keep in camp, or risk *mal de raquette,*—strain of legs by heavy snow-shoeing. So they were in great haste to make the best of fine weather.

Tom thrust his Jacob's-staff into the snow, set the compass sights to the right bearing, looked through them, and stood by to let Big Baptiste get a course along the line ahead. Baptiste's duty was to walk straight for some selected object far away on the line. In wood-land the axeman "blazed" trees on both sides of his snow-shoe track.

Baptiste was as expert at his job as any Indian, and indeed he looked as if he had a streak of Iroquois in his veins. So did "Frawce," "Jawnny," and all their comrades of the party.

"The three pines will do," said Tom, as Baptiste crouched.

"Good luck to-day for sure!" cried Baptiste, rising with his eyes fixed on three pines in the foreground of the distant timbered ridge. He saw that the line did indeed run clear of trees for two miles along one side of the long, narrow beaver meadow or swale.

Baptiste drew a deep breath, and grinned agreeably at Tom Dunscombe.

"De boys will look like dey's all got de double pay in deys' pocket when dey's see *dis* open," said Baptiste, and started for the three pines as straight as a bee.

Tom waited to get from the chainmen the distance to the edge of the wood. They came on the heels of the axemen, and all capered on their snow-shoes to see so long a space free from cutting.

It was now two o'clock; they had marched with forty pound or "light" packs since daylight, lunching on cold pork and hard-tack as they worked; they had slept cold for weeks on brush under an open tent pitched over a hole in the snow; they must live this life of hardship and huge work for six weeks longer, but they hoped to get twice their usual eighty-cents-a-day pay, and so their hearts were light and jolly.

But Big Baptiste, now two hundred yards in advance, swinging along in full view of the party, stopped with a scared cry. They saw him look to the left and to the right, and over his shoulder behind, like a man who expects mortal attack from a near but unknown quarter.

"What's the matter?" shouted Tom.

Baptiste went forward a few steps, hesitated, stopped, turned, and fairly ran back toward the party. As he came he continually turned his head from side to side as if expecting to see some dreadful thing following.

The men behind Tom stopped. Their faces were blanched. They looked, too, from side to side.

"Halt, Mr. Tom, halt! Oh, *monjee*, M'sieu, stop!" said Jawnny.

Tom looked round at his men, amazed at their faces of mysterious terror.

"What on earth has happened?" cried he.

Instead of answering, the men simply pointed to Big Baptiste who was soon within twenty yards.

"What is the trouble, Baptiste?" asked Tom.

Baptiste's face was the hue of death. As he spoke he shuddered:—

"*Monjee*, Mr. Tom, we'll got for stop de job!"

"Stop the job! Are you crazy?"

"If you'll not b'lieve what I told, den you go'n' see for you'se'f."

"What is it?"

"De track, seh."

"What track? Wolves?"

"If it was only wolfs!"

"Confound you! can't you say what it is?"

"Eet's de—it ain't safe for told its name out loud, for dass de way it come—if it's call by its name!"

"Windego, eh?" said Tom, laughing.

"I'll know its track jus' as quick's I see it."

"Do you mean you have seen a Windego track?"

"Monjee, seh, *don't* say its name! Let us go back," said Jawnny. "Baptiste was at Madores' shanty with us when it took Hermidas Dubois."

"Yesseh. That's de way I'll come for know de track soon's I see it," said Baptiste. "Before den I mos' don' b'lieve dere was any of it. But ain't it take Hermidas Dubois only last New Year's?"

"That was all nonsense about Dubois. I'll bet it was a joke to scare you all."

"Who's kill a man for a joke?" said Baptiste.

"Did you see Hermidas Dubois killed? Did you see him dead? No! I heard all about it. All you know is that he went away on New Year's morning, when the rest of the men were too scared to leave the shanty, because someone said there was a Windego track outside."

"Hermidas never come back!"

"I'll bet he went away home. You'll find him at Saint Agathe in the spring. You can't be such fools as to believe in Windegos."

"Don't you say dat name some more!" yelled Big Baptiste, now fierce with fright. "Hain't I just seen de track? I'm go'n' back, me, if I don't get a copper of pay for de whole winter!"

"Wait a little now, Baptiste," said Tom, alarmed lest his party should desert him and the job. "I'll soon find out what's at the bottom of the track."

Dere is blood at de bottom—I seen it!" said Baptiste.

"Well, you wait till *I* go and see it."

"No! I go back, me," said Baptiste, and started up the slope with the others at his heels.

"Halt! Stop there! Halt, you fools! Don't you understand that if there was any such monster it would as easily catch you in one place as another?"

The men went on. Tom took another tone.

"Boys, look here! I say, are you going to desert me like cowards?"

"Hain't goin' for desert you, Mr. Tom, no seh!" said Baptiste, halting. "Honly I'll hain' go for cross de track." They all faced round.

Tom was acquainted with a considerable number of Windego superstitions.

"There's no danger unless it's a fresh track," he said. "Perhaps it's an old one."

"Fresh made dis mornin'," said Baptiste.

"Well, wait till I go and see it. You're all right, you know, if you don't cross it. Isn't that the idea?"

"No, seh. Mr. Humphreys told Madore 'bout dat. Eef somebody cross de track and don't never come back, *den* de magic ain't in de track no more. But it's watchin', watchin' all round to catch somebody what cross its track; and if nobody don't cross its track and get catched, den de—de *Ting* mebby get crazy mad, and nobody don' know what it's goin' for do. Kill every person, mebby."

Tom mused over this information. These men had all been in Madore's shanty; Madore was under Red Dick Humphreys; Red Dick was Rory Carmichael's head foreman; he had sworn to stop the survey by hook or by crook, and this vow had been made after Tom had hired his gang from among those scared away from Madore's shanty. Tom thought he began to understand the situation.

"Just wait a bit, boys," he said, and started.

"You ain't surely go'n for cross de track?" cried Baptiste.

"Not now, anyway," said Tom. "But wait till I see it."

When he reached the mysterious track it surprised him so greatly that he easily forgave Baptiste's fears.

If a giant having ill-shaped feet as long as Tom's snow-shoes had passed by in moccasins, the main features of the indentations might have been produced. But the marks were no deeper in the snow than if the huge moccasins had been worn by an ordinary man. They were about five and a half feet apart from centres, a stride that no human legs could take at a walking pace.

Moreover, there were on the snow none of the dragging marks of striding; the gigantic feet had apparently been lifted straight up clear of the snow, and put straight down.

Strangest of all, at the front of each print were five narrow holes which suggested that the mysterious creature had travelled with bare, claw-like toes. An irregular drip or squirt of blood went along the middle of the indentations! Nevertheless, the whole thing seemed of human devising.

This track, Tom reflected, was consistent with the Indian superstition that Windegos are monsters who take on or relinquish the human form, and vary their size at pleasure. He perceived that he must bring the maker of those tracks promptly to book, or suffer his men to desert the survey, and cost him his whole winter's work, besides making him a laughing-stock in the settlements.

The young fellow made his decision instantly. After feeling for his match-box and sheath-knife, he took his hatchet from his sash, and called to the men.

"Go into camp and wait for me!"

Then he set off alongside of the mysterious track at his best pace. It came out of a tangle of alders to the west, and went into such another tangle about a quarter of a mile to the east. Tom went east. The men watched him with horror.

"He's got crazy, looking at de track," said Big Baptiste, "for that's the way,—one is enchanted,—he must follow."

"He was a good boss," said Jawnny, sadly.

As the young fellow disappeared in the alders the men looked at one another with a certain shame. Not a sound except the sough of pines from the neighboring forest was heard. Though the sun was sinking in clear blue, the aspect of the wilderness, gray and white and severe, touched the impressionable men with deeper melancholy. They felt lonely, masterless, mean.

"He was a good boss," said Jawnny again.

"Tort Dieu!" cried Baptiste, leaping to his feet. "It's a shame for desert the young boss. I don't care; the Windego can only kill me. I'm going for help Mr. Tom."

"Me also," said Jawnny.

Then all wished to go. But after some parley it was agreed that the others should wait for the portageurs, who were likely to be two miles behind, and make camp for the night.

Soon Baptiste and Jawnny, each with his axe, started diagonally across the swale, and entered the alders on Tom's track.

It took them twenty yards through the alders, to the edge of a warm spring or marsh about fifty yards wide. This open, shallow water was completely encircled by alders that came down to its very edge. Tom's snow-shoe track joined the track of the mysterious monster for the first time on the edge—and there both vanished!

Baptiste and Jawnny looked at the place with the wildest terror, and without even thinking to search the deeply indented opposite edges of the little pool for a reappearance of the tracks, fled back to the party. It was just as Red Dick Humphreys had said; just as they had always heard. Tom, like Hermidas Dubois, appeared to have vanished from existence the moment he stepped on the Windego track!

The dimness of early evening was in the red-pine forest through which Tom's party had passed early in the afternoon, and the belated portageurs were tramping along the line. A man with a red head had been long crouching in some cedar bushes to the east of the "blazed" cutting. When he had watched the portageurs pass out of sight, he stepped over upon their track, and followed it a short distance.

A few minutes later a young fellow, over six feet high, who strongly resembled Tom Dunscombe, followed the red-headed man.

The stranger, suddenly catching sight of a flame far away ahead on the edge of the beaver meadow, stopped and fairly hugged himself.

"Camped, by jiminy! I knowed I'd fetch 'em," was the only remark he made.

"I wish Big Baptiste could see that Windego laugh," thought Tom Dunscombe, concealed behind a tree.

After reflecting a few moments, the red-headed man, a wiry little fellow, went forward till he came to where an old snow-shoes had recently fallen across the track. There he kicked off his snow-shoes, picked them up, ran along the trunk, jumped into the snow from among the branches, put on his snow-shoes, and started northwestward. His new track could not be seen from the survey line.

But Tom had beheld and understood the purpose of the manoeuvre. He made straight for the head of the fallen tree, got on the stranger's tracks and cautiously followed them, keeping far enough behind to be out of hearing or sight.

The red-headed stranger went toward the wood out of which the mysterious track of the morning had come. When he had reached the little brush-camp in which he had slept the previous night, he made a small fire, put a small tin pot on it, boiled some tea, broiled a venison steak, ate his supper, had several good laughs, took a long smoke, rolled himself round and round in his blanket, and went to sleep.

Hours passed before Tom ventured to crawl forward and peer into the brush camp. The red-headed man was lying on his face, as is the custom of many woodsmen. His capuchin cap covered his red head.

Tom Dunscombe took off his own long sash. When the red-headed man woke up he found that some one was on his back, holding his head firmly down.

Unable to extricate his arms or legs from his blankets, the red-headed man began to utter fearful threats. Tom said not one word, but diligently wound his sash round his prisoner's head, shoulders, and arms.

He then rose, took the red-headed man's own "tump-line," a leather strap about twelve feet long, which tapered from the middle to both ends, tied this firmly round the angry live mummy, and left him lying on his face.

Then, collecting his prisoner's axe, snow-shoes, provisions, and tin pail, Tom started with them back along the Windego track for camp.

Big Baptiste and his comrades had supped too full of fears to go to sleep. They had built an enormous fire, because Windegos are reported, in Indian circles, to share with wild beasts the dread of flames and brands. Tom stole quietly to within fifty yards of the camp, and suddenly shouted in unearthly fashion. The men sprang up, quaking.

"It's the Windego!" screamed Jawnny.

"You silly fools!" said Tom, coming forward. "Don't you know my voice? Am I a Windego?"

"It's the Windego, for sure; it's took the shape of Mr. Tom, after eatin' him," cried Big Baptiste.

Tom laughed so uproariously at this that the other men scouted the idea, though it was quite in keeping with their information concerning Windegos' habits.

Then Tom came in and gave a full and particular account of the Windego's pursuit, capture, and present predicament.

"But how'd he make de track?" they asked.

"He had two big old snow-shoes, stuffed with spruce tips underneath, and covered with dressed deerskin. He had cut off the back ends of them. You shall see them to-morrow. I found them down yonder where he had left them after crossing the warm spring. He had five bits of sharp round wood going down in front of them. He must have stood on them one after the other, and lifted the back one every time with the pole he carried. I've got that, too. The blood was from a deer he had run down and killed in the snow. He carried the blood in his tin pail, and sprinkled it behind him. He must have run out our line long ago with a compass, so he knew where it would go. But come, let us go and see if it's Red Dick Humphreys."

Red Dick proved to be the prisoner. He had become quite philosophic while waiting for his captor to come back. When unbound he grinned pleasantly, and remarked:

"You're Mr. Dunscombe, eh? Well, you're a smart young feller, Mr. Dunscombe. There ain't another man on the Ottaway that could 'a' done that trick on me. Old Dan McEachran will make your fortun' for this, and I don't begrudge it. You're a man— that's so. If ever I hear any feller saying to the contrayry he's got to lick Red Dick Humphreys."

And he told them the particulars of his practical joke in making a Windego track round Madore's shanty.

"Hermidas Dubois?—oh, he's all right," said Red Dick. "He's at home at St. Agathe. Man, he helped me to fix up that Windego track at Madore's, but, by criminy! the look of it scared him so he wouldn't cross it himself. It was a holy terror!"

Little Baptiste

Ottawa River

Ma'ame Baptiste Larocque peered again into her cupboard and her flour barrel, as though she might have been mistaken in her inspection twenty minutes earlier.

"No, there is nothing, nothing at all!" said she to her old mother-in-law. "And no more trust at the store. Monsieur Conolly was too cross when I went for corn-meal yesterday. For sure, Baptiste stays very long at the shanty this year."

"Fear nothing, Delima," answered the bright-eyed old woman. "The good God will send a breakfast for the little ones, and for us. In seventy years I do not know Him to fail once, my daughter. Baptiste may be back tomorrow, and with more money for staying so long. No, no; fear not, Delima! *Le bon Dieu* manages all for the best."

"That is true; for so I have heard always," answered Delima, with conviction; "but sometimes *le bon Dieu* requires one's inside to pray very loud. Certainly I trust, like you, *Memere;* but it would be pleasant if He would send the food the day before."

"Ah, you are too anxious, like little Baptiste here," and the old woman glanced at the boy sitting by the cradle. "Young folks did not talk so when I was little. Then we did not think there was danger in trusting *Monsieur le Curé* when he told us to take no heed of the morrow. But now! to hear them talk, one might think they had never heard of *le bon Dieu*. The young people think too much, for sure. Trust in the good God, I say. Breakfast and dinner and supper too we shall all have to-morrow."

"Yes, *Memere,*" replied the boy, who was called little Baptiste to distinguish him from his father. *"Le bon Dieu* will send an excellent breakfast, sure enough, If I get up very early, and find some good *doré* (pickerel) and catfish on the night-line. But if I did not bait the hooks, what then? Well, I hope there will be more to-morrow than this morning, anyway."

"There were enough," said the old woman, severely. "Have we not had plenty all day, Delima?"

Delima made no answer. She was in doubt about the plenty which her mother-in-law spoke of. She wondered whether small André and Odillon and 'Toinette, whose heavy breathing she could hear through the thin partition, would have been sleeping so peacefully had little Baptiste not divided his share among them at supper-time, with the excuse that he did not feel very well?

Delima was young yet,—though little Baptiste was such a big boy, —and would have rested fully on the positively expressed trust of her mother-in-law, in spite of the empty flour barrel, if she had not suspected little Baptiste of sitting there hungry.

However, he was such a strange boy, she soon reflected, that perhaps going empty did not make him feel bad! Little Baptiste was so decided in his ways, made what in others would have been sacrifices so much as a matter of course, and was so much disgusted on being offered credit or sympathy in consequence, that his mother, not being able to understand him, was not a little afraid of him.

He was not very formidable in appearance, however, that clumsy boy of fourteen or so, whose big freckled, good face was now bent over the cradle where *la petite* Seraphine lay smiling in her sleep, with soft little fingers clutched round his rough one.

"For sure," said Delima, observing the baby's smile, "the good angels are very near. I wonder what they are telling her?"

"Something about her father, of course; for so I have always heard it is when the infants smile in sleep," answered the old woman.

Little Baptiste rose impatiently and went into the sleeping-room. Often the simplicity and sentimentality of his mother and grandmother gave him strange pangs at heart; they seemed to be the children, while he felt very old. They were always looking for wonderful things to happen, and expecting the saints and *le bon Dieu* to help the family out of difficulties that little Baptiste saw no way of overcoming without the work which was then so hard to get. His mother's remark about the angels talking to little Seraphine pained him so much that he would have cried had he not felt compelled to be very much of a man during his father's absence.

If he had been asked to name the spirit hovering about, he would have mentioned a very wicked one as personified in John Conolly, the village storekeeper, the vampire of the little hamlet a quarter of a mile distant. Conolly owned the tavern too, and a sawmill up river, and altogether was a very rich, powerful, and dreadful person in little Baptiste's view. Worst of all, he practically owned the cabin and lot of the Larocques, for he had made big Baptiste give him a bill of sale of the place as security for groceries to be advanced to the family while its head was away in the shanty; and that afternoon Conolly had said to little Baptiste that the credit had been exhausted, and more.

"No; you can't get any pork," said the storekeeper. "Don't your mother know that, after me sending her away when she wanted corn-meal yesterday? Tell her she don't get another cent's worth here."

"For why not? My fader always he pay," said the indignant boy, trying to talk English.

"Yes, indeed! Well, he ain't paid this time. How do I know what's happened to him, as he ain't back from the shanty? Tell you what: I'm going to turn you all out if your mother don't pay rent in advance for the shanty tomorrow,—four dollars a month."

"What you talkin' so for? We doan' goin' pay no rent for our own house!"

"You doan' goin' to own no house," answered Conolly, mimicking the boy. "The house is mine any time I like to say so. If the store bill ain't paid to-night, out you go tomorrow, or else pay rent. Tell your mother that for me. Mosey off now. '*Marche, donc!*' There's no other way."

Little Baptiste had not told his mother of this terrible threat, for what was the use? She had no money. He knew that she would begin weeping and wailing, with small André and Odillon as a puzzled, excited chorus, with 'Toinette and Seraphine adding those baby cries that made little Baptiste want to cry himself; with his grandmother steadily advising, in the din, that patient trust in *le bon Dieu* which he could not always entertain, though he felt very wretched that he could not.

Moreover, he desired to spare his mother and grandmother as long as possible. "Let them have their good night's sleep," said he to himself, with such thoughtfulness and pity as a merchant might feel in concealing imminent bankruptcy from his family. He knew there was but one chance remaining,—that his father might come home during the night or next morning, with his winter's wages.

Big Baptiste had "gone up" for Rewbell the jobber; had gone in November, to make logs in the distant Petawawa woods, and now the month was May. The "very magnificent" pig he had salted down before going away had been eaten long ago. My! what a time it seemed now to little Baptiste since that pig-killing! How good the *boudin* (the blood-puddings) had been, and the liver and tender bits, and what a joyful time they had had! The barrelful of salted pike and catfish was all gone too,—which made the fact that the fish were not biting well this year very sad indeed.

Now on top of all these troubles this new danger of being turned out on the roadside! For where are they to get four dollars, or two, or one even, to stave Conolly off? Certainly his father was away too long; but surely, surely, thought the boy, he would get back in time to save his home! Then he remembered with horror, and a feeling of being disloyal to his father for remembering, that terrible day, three years before, when big Baptiste had come back from his winter's work drunk, and without a dollar, having been robbed while on a spree in Ottawa. If that were the reason of his father's delay now, ah, then there would be no hope, unless *le bon Dieu* should indeed work a miracle for them!

While the boy thought over the situation with fear, his grandmother went to her bed, and soon afterward Delima took the little Seraphine's cradle into the sleeping-room. That left little Baptiste so lonely that he could not sit still; nor did he see any use of going to lie awake in bed by André and Odillon.

So he left the cabin softly, and reaching the river with a few steps, pushed off his flat-bottomed boat, and was carried smartly up stream by the shore eddy. It soon gave him to the current, and then he drifted idly down under the bright moon, listening to the roar of the long rapid, near the foot of which their cabin stood. Then he took to his oars, and rowed to the end of his night-line, tied to the wharf. He had an unusual fear that it might be gone, but found it all right, stretched taut; a slender rope, four hundred feet long, floated here and there far away in the darkness by flat cedar sticks,—a rope carrying short bits of line, and forty hooks, all loaded with excellent fat, wriggling worms.

That day little Baptiste had taken much trouble with his night-line; he was proud of the plentiful bait, and now, as he felt the tightened rope with his fingers, he told himself that his well-filled hooks *must* attract plenty of fish,—perhaps a sturgeon! Wouldn't that be grand? A big sturgeon of seventy-five pounds!

He pondered the Ottawa statement that "there are seven kinds of meat on the head of a sturgeon," and, enumerating the kinds, fell into a conviction that one sturgeon at least would surely come to his line. Had not three been caught in one night by Pierre Mallette, who had no sort of claim, who was too lazy to bait more than half his hooks, altogether too wicked to receive any special favors from *le bon Dieu?*

Little Baptiste rowed home, entered the cabin softly, and stripped for bed, almost happy in guessing what the big fish would probably weigh.

Putting his arms around little André, he tried to go to sleep; but the threats of Conolly came to him with new force, and he lay awake, with a heavy dread in his heart.

How long he had been lying thus he did not know, when a heavy step came upon the plank outside the door.

"Father's home!" cried little Baptiste, springing to the floor as the door opened.

"Baptiste! my own Baptiste!" cried Delima, putting her arms around her husband as he stood over her.

"Did I not say," said the old woman, seizing her son's hand, "that the good God would send help in time?"

Little Baptiste lit they lamp. Then they saw something in the father's face that startled them all. He had not spoken, and now they perceived that he was haggard, pale, wild-eyed.

"The good God!" cried big Baptiste, and knelt by the bed, and bowed his head on his arms, and wept so loudly that little André and Odillon, wakening, joined his cry. *"Le bon Dieu* has forgotten us! For all my winter's work I have not one dollar! The concern is failed. Rewbell paid not one cent of wages, but ran away, and the timber has been seized."

Oh, the heartbreak! Oh, poor Delima! poor children! and poor little Baptiste, with the threats of Conolly rending his heart!

"I have walked all day," said the father, "and eaten not a thing. Give me something, Delima."

"O holy angels!" cried the poor woman, breaking into a wild weeping. "O Baptiste, Baptiste, my poor man! There is nothing; not a scrap; not any flour, not meal, not grease even; not a pinch of tea!" but still she searched frantically about the rooms.

"Never mind," said big Baptiste then, holding her in his strong arms. "I am not so hungry as tired, Delima, and I can sleep."

The old woman, who had been swaying to and fro in her chair of rushes, rose now, and laid her aged hands on the broad shoulders of the man.

"My son Baptiste," she said, "you must not say that God has forgotten us, for He has not forgotten us. The hunger is hard to bear, I know,—hard, hard to bear; but great plenty will be sent in answer to our prayers. And it is hard, hard to lose thy long winter's work; but be patient, my son, and thankful, yes, thankful for all thou hast.

"Behold, Delima is well and strong. See the little Baptiste, how much a man! Yes, that is right; kiss the little André and Odillon; and see! how sweetly 'Toinette sleeps! All strong and well, son Baptiste! Were one gone, think what thou wouldst have lost! But instead, be thankful, for behold, another has been given,— the little Seraphine here, that thou has not before seen!"

Big, rough, soft-hearted Baptiste knelt by the cradle, and kissed the babe gently.

"It is true, *Memere,*" he answered, "and I thank *le bon Dieu* for his goodness to me."

But little Baptiste, lying wide awake for hours afterwards, was not thankful. He could not see that matters could be much worse. A big hard lump was in his throat as he thought of his father's hunger, and the home-coming so different from what they had fondly counted on. Great slow tears came into the boy's eyes, and he wiped them away, ashamed even in the dark to have been guilty of such weakness.

In the gray dawn little Baptiste suddenly awoke, with the sensation of having slept on his post. How heavy his heart was! Why? He sat dazed with indefinite sorrow. Ah, now he remembered! Conolly threatening to turn them out! and his father back penniless! No breakfast! Well, we must see about that.

Very quietly he rose, put on his patched clothes, and went out. Heavy mist covered the face of the river, and somehow the rapid seemed stilled to a deep, pervasive murmur. As he pushed his boat off, the morning fog was chillier than frost about him; but his heart got lighter as he rowed toward his night-line, and he became even eager for the pleasure of handling his fish. He made up his mind not to be much disappointed if there were no sturgeon, but could not quite believe there would be none; surely it was reasonable to expect *one*, perhaps two— why not three?—among the catfish and *doré*.

How very taut and heavy the rope felt as he raised it over his gunwales, and letting the bow swing up stream, began pulling in the line hand over hand! He had heard of cases where every hook had its fish; such a thing might happen again surely! Yard after yard of rope he passed slowly over the boat, and down into the water it sank on his track.

Now a knot on the line told him he was nearing the first hook; he watched for the quiver and struggle of the fish,—probably a big one, for there he had put a tremendous bait on and spat on it for luck, moreover. What? the short line hung down from the rope, and the baited hook rose clear of the water!

Baptiste instantly made up his mind that that hook had been placed a little too far inshore; he remembered thinking so before; the next hook was in about the right place!

Hand over hand, ah! the second hook, too! Still baited, the big worm very livid! It must be thus because that worm was pushed up the shank of the hook in such a queer way: he had been rather pleased when he gave the bait that particular twist, and now was surprised at himself; why, any one could see it was a thing to scare fish!

Hand over hand to the third,—the hook was naked of bait! Well, that was more satisfactory; it showed they had been biting, and after all, this was just about the beginning of the right place.

Hand over hand; *now* the splashing will begin, thought little Baptiste, and out came the fourth hook with its livid worm! He held the rope in his hand without drawing it in for a few moments, but could see no reasonable objection to that last worm. His heart sank a little, but pshaw! only four hooks out of forty were up yet! wait till the eddy behind the shoal was reached, then great things would be seen. Maybe the fish had not been lying in that first bit of current.

Hand over hand again, now! yes, certainly, *there* is the right swirl! What? a *losch*, that unclean semi-lizard! The boy tore if off and flung it indignantly into the river. However, there was good luck in a *losch;* that was well known.

But the next hook, and the next, and next, and next came up baited and fishless. He pulled hand over hand quickly—not a fish! and he must have gone over half the line! Little Baptiste stopped, with his heart like lead and his arms trembling. It was terrible! Not a fish, and his father had no supper, and there was no credit at the store. Poor little Baptiste!

Again he hauled hand over hand—one hook, two, three—oh! ho! Glorious! What a delightful sheer downward the rope took! Surely the big sturgeon at last, trying to stay down on the bottom with the hook! But Baptiste would show that fish his mistake. He pulled, pulled, stood up to pull; there was a sort of shake, a sudden give of the rope, and little Baptiste tumbled over backward as he jerked his line up from under the big stone!

Then he heard the shutters clattering as Conolly's clerk took them off the store window; at half-past five to the minute that was always done. Soon big Baptiste would be up, that was certain. Again the boy began hauling in line: baited hook! baited hook! naked hook! baited hook!—such was still the tale.

"Surely, surely," implored little Baptiste, silently, "I shall find some fish!" Up! up! only four remained! The boy broke down. Could it be? Had he not somehow skipped many hooks? Could it be that there was to be no breakfast for the children? Naked hook again! Oh, for some fish! anything! three, two!

"Oh, send just one for my father!—my poor, hungry father!" cried little Baptiste, and drew up his last hook. It came full baited, and the line was out of the water clear away to his outer buoy!

He let go the rope and drifted down the river, crying as though his heart would break. All the good hooks useless! all the labor thrown away! all his self-confidence come to naught!

Up rose the great sun; from around the kneeling boy drifted the last of the morning mists; bright beams touched his bowed head tenderly. He lifted his face and looked up the rapid. Then he jumped to his feet with sudden wonder; a great joy lit up his countenance.

Far up the river a low, broad, white patch appeared on the sharp sky-line made by the level dark summit of the long slope of tumbling water. On this white patch stood many figures of swaying men black against the clear morning sky, and little Baptiste saw instantly that an attempt was being made to "run" a "band" of deals, or many cribs lashed together, instead of single cribs as had been done the day before.

The broad strip of white changed its form slowly, dipped over the slope, drew out like a wide ribbon, and soon showed a distinct slant across the mighty volume of the deep raft channel. When little Baptiste, acquainted as he was with every current, eddy, and shoal in the rapid, saw that slant, he knew that his first impression of what was about to happen had been correct. The pilot of the band *had* allowed it to drift too far north before reaching the rapid's head.

Now the front cribs, instead of following the curve of the channel, had taken slower water, while the rear cribs, impelled by the rush under them, swung the band slowly across the current. All along the front the standing men swayed back and forth, plying sweeps full forty feet long, attempting to swing into channel again, with their strokes dashing the dark rollers before the band into wide splashes of white. On the rear cribs another crew pulled in the contrary direction; about the middle of the band stood the pilot, urging his gangs with gestures to greater efforts.

Suddenly he made a new motion; the gang behind drew in their oars and ran hastily forward to double the force in front. But they came too late! Hardly had the doubled bow crew taken a stroke when all drew in their oars and ran back to be out of danger. Next moment the front cribs struck the "hog's-back" shoal.

Then the long broad band curved downward in the centre, the rear cribs swung into the shallows on the opposite side of the raft-channel, there was a great straining and crashing, the men in front huddled together, watching the wreck anxiously, and the band went speedily to pieces. Soon a fringe of single planks came down stream, then cribs and pieces of cribs; half the band was drifting with the currents, and half was "hung up" on the rocks among the breakers.

Launching the big red flat-bottomed bow boat, twenty of the raftsmen came with wild speed down the river, and as there had been no rush to get aboard, little Baptiste knew that the cribs on which the men stood were so hard aground that no lives were in danger. It meant much to him; it meant that he was instantly at liberty to gather in *money!* money, in sums that loomed to gigantic figures before his imagination.

He knew that there was an important reason for hurrying the deals to Quebec, else the great risk of running a band at that season would not have been undertaken; and he knew that hard cash would be paid down as salvage for all planks brought ashore, and thus secured from drifting far and wide over the lake-like expanse below the rapid's foot. Little Baptiste plunged his oars in and made for a clump of deals floating in the eddy near his own shore. As he rushed along, the raftsmen's boat crossed his bows, going to the main raft below for ropes and material to secure the cribs coming down intact.

"Good boy!" shouted the foreman to Baptiste. "Ten cents for every deal you fetch ashore above the raft!"

Ten cents! he had expected but five! What a harvest!

Striking his pike-pole into the clump of deals,—"fifty at least," said joyful Baptiste,—he soon secured them to his boat, and then pulled, pulled, pulled, till the blood rushed to his head, and his arms ached, before he landed his wealth.

"Father!" cried he, bursting breathlessly into the sleeping household. "Come quick! I can't get it up without you."

"Big sturgeon?" cried the shantyman, jumping into his trousers.

"Oh, but we shall have a good fish breakfast!" cried Delima.

"Did I not say the blessed *le bon Dieu* would send plenty fish?" observed *Memere.*

"Not a fish!" cried little Baptiste, with recovered breath. "But look! look!" and he flung open the door. The eddy was now white with planks.

"Ten cents for each!" cried the boy. "The foreman told me."

"Ten cents!" shouted his father. "*Baptême!* it's my winter's wages!"

And the old grandmother! And Delima? Why, they just put their arms round each other and cried for joy.

"And yet there's no breakfast," said Delima, starting up. "And they will work hard, hard."

At that instant who should reach the door but Monsieur Conolly! He was a man who respected cash wherever he found it, and already the two Baptistes had a fine show ashore.

"Ma'ame Larocque," said Conolly, politely, putting in his head, "of course you know I was only joking yesterday. You can get anything you want at the store."

What a breakfast they did have, to be sure! the Baptistes eating while they worked. Back and forward they dashed till late afternoon, driving ringed spikes into the deals, running light ropes through the rings, and, when a good string had thus been made, going ashore to haul in. At that hauling Delima and *Memere,* even little André and Odillon gave a hand.

Everybody in the little hamlet made money that day, but the Larocques twice as much as any other family, because they had an eddy and a low shore. With the help of the people "the big *Bourgeois*" who owned the broken raft got it away that evening, and saved his fat contract after all.

"Did I not say so?" said "*Memere,*" at night for the hundredth time. "Did I not say so? Yes, indeed, *le bon Dieu* watches over us all."

"Yes, indeed, grandmother," echoed little Baptiste, thinking of his failure on the nightline. "We may take as much trouble as we like, but it's no use unless *le bon Dieu* helps us. Only—I don't know what de big Bourgeois say about that—his raft was all broke up so bad."

"Ah, *oui,*" said *Memere,* looking puzzled for but a moment. "But he didn't put his trust in *le bon Dieu;* that's it, for sure. Besides, maybe *le bon Dieu* want to teach him a lesson; he'll not try for run a whole band of deals next time. You see that was a tempting of Providence; and then—the big Bourgeois is a Protestant."

The Waterloo Veteran

Is Waterloo a dead word to you? the name of a plain of battle, no more? Or do you see, on a space of rising ground, the little long-coated man with marble features, and unquenchable eyes that pierce through rolling smoke to where the relics of the old Guard of France stagger and rally and reach fiercely again up the hill of St. Jean toward the squares, set, torn, red, re-formed, stubborn, mangled, victorious beneath the unflinching will of him behind there,—the Iron Duke of England?

Or is your interest in the fight literary? and do you see in a pause of the conflict Major O'Dowd sitting on the carcass of Pyramus refreshing himself from that case-bottle of sound brandy? George Osborne lying yonder, all his fopperies ended, with a bullet through his heart? Rawdon Crawley riding stolidly behind General Tufto along the front of the shattered regiment where Captain Dobbin stands heartsick for poor Emily?

Or maybe the struggle arranges itself in your vision around one figure not named in history or fiction,—that of your grandfather, or his father, or some old dead soldier of the great wars whose blood you exult to inherit, or some grim veteran whom you saw tottering to the rollcall beyond when Queen Victoria was young and you were a little boy.

For me the shadows of the battle are so grouped round old John Locke that the historians, story-tellers, and painters may never quite persuade me that he was not the centre and real hero of the action. The French cuirassiers in my thought-pictures charge again and again vainly against old John; he it is who breaks the New Guard; upon the ground that he defends the Emperor's eyes are fixed all day long. It is John who occasionally glances at the sky with wonder if Blucher has failed them. Upon Shaw the Lifeguardsman, and John, the Duke plainly most relies, and the words that Wellington actually speaks when the time comes for advance are, "Up, John, and at them!"

How fate drifted the old veteran of Waterloo into our little Canadian Lake Erie village I never knew. Drifted him? No; he ever marched as if under the orders of his commander. Tall, thin, white-haired, close-shaven, and always in knee-breeches and long stockings, his was an antique and martial figure. "Fresh white-fish" was his cry, which he delivered as if calling all the village to fall in for drill.

So impressive was his demeanor that he dignified his occupation. For years after he disappeared, the peddling of white-fish by horse and cart was regarded in that district as peculiarly respectable. It was a glorious trade when old John Locke held the steelyards and served out the glittering fish with an air of distributing ammunition for a long day's combat.

I believe I noticed, on the first day I saw him, how he tapped his left breast with a proud gesture when he had done with a lot of customers and was about to march again at the head of his horse. That restored him from trade to his soldiership—he had saluted his Waterloo medal! There beneath his threadbare old blue coat it lay, always felt by the heart of the hero.

"Why doesn't he wear it outside?" I once asked.

"He used to," said my father; "till Hiram Beaman, the druggist, asked him what he'd 'take for the bit of pewter.' "

"What did old John say, sir?"

" 'Take for the bit of pewter!' said he, looking hard at Beaman with scorn. 'I've took better men's lives nor ever yours was for to get it, and I'd sell my own for it as quick as ever I offered it before.'

" 'More fool you,' said Beaman.

" 'You're nowt,' said old John, very calm and cold, 'you're nowt but walking dirt.' From that day forth he would never sell Beaman a fish; he wouldn't touch his money."

It must have been late in 1854 or early in 1855 that I first saw the famous medal. Going home from school on a bright winter afternoon, I met old John walking very erect, without his usual fish-supply. A dull round white spot was clasped on the left breast of his coat.

"Mr. Locke," said the small boy, staring with admiration, "is that your glorious Waterloo medal?"

"You're a good little lad!" He stooped to let me see the noble pewter. "War's declared against Rooshia, and now it's right to show it. The old regiment's sailed, and my only son is with the colors."

Then he took me by the hand and led me into the village store, where the lawyer read aloud the news from the paper that the veteran gave him. In those days there was no railway within fifty miles of us. It had chanced that some fisherman brought old John a later paper than any previously received in the village.

"Ay, but the Duke is gone," said he shaking his white head, "and it's curious to be fighting on the same side with another Boney."

All that winter and the next, all the long summer between, old John displayed his medal. When the report of Alma came, his remarks on the French failure to get into the fight were severe. "What was they ever, at best, without Boney?" he would inquire. But a letter from his son after Inkermann changed all that.

"Half of us was killed, and the rest of us clean tired with fighting," wrote Corporal Locke. "What with a bullet through the flesh of my right leg, and the fatigue of using the bayonet so long, I was like to drop. The Russians was coming on again as if there was no end to them, when strange drums came sounding in the mist behind us. With that we closed up and faced half-round, thinking they had outflanked us and the day was gone, so there was nothing more to do but make out to die hard, like the sons of Waterloo men. You would have been pleased to see the looks of what was left of the old regiment, father. Then all of a sudden a French column came up the rise out of the mist, screaming, '*Vive l'Empereur!*' their drums beating the charge. We gave them room, for we were too dead tired to go first. On they went like mad at the Russians, so that was the end of a hard morning's work. I was down,—fainted with loss of blood,—but I will soon be fit for duty again. When I came to myself there was a Frenchman pouring brandy down my throat, and talking in his gibberish as kind as any Christian. Never a word will I say agin them red-legged French again."

"Show me the man that would!" growled old John. "It was never in them French to act cowardly. Didn't they beat all the world, and even stand up many's the day agen ourselves and the Duke? They didn't beat,—it wouldn't be in reason,—but they tried brave enough, and what more'd you ask of mortal men?"

With the ending of the Crimean War our village was illuminated. Rows of tallow candles in every window, fireworks in a vacant field, and a torchlight procession! Old John marched at its head in full regimentals, straight as a ramrod, the hero of the night. His son had been promoted for bravery on the field. After John came a dozen gray militiamen of Queenston Heights, Lundy's Lane, and Chippewa; next some forty volunteers of '37. And we boys of the U.E. Loyalist settlement cheered and cheered, thrilled with an intense vague knowledge that the old army of Wellington kept ghostly step with John, while aerial trumpets and drums pealed and beat with rejoicing at the fresh glory of the race and the union of English-speaking men unconsciously celebrated and symbolized by the little rustic parade.

After that the old man again wore his medal concealed. The Chinese War of 1857 was too contemptible to celebrate by displaying his badge of Waterloo.

Then came the dreadful tale of the Sepoy mutiny—Meerut, Delhi, Cawnpore! After the tale of Nana Sahib's massacre of women and children was read to old John he never smiled, I think. Week after week, month after month, as hideous tidings poured steadily in, his face became more haggard, gray, and dreadful. The feeling that he was too old for use seemed to shame him. He no longer carried his head high, as of yore. That his son was not marching behind Havelock with the avenging army seemed to cut our veteran sorely. Sergeant Locke had sailed with the old regiment to join Outram in Persia before the Sepoys broke loose. It was at this time that old John was first heard to say, "I'm 'feared something's gone wrong with my heart."

Months went by before we learned that the troops for Persia had been stopped on their way and thrown into India against the mutineers. At that news old John marched into the village with a prouder air than he had worn for many a day. His medal was again on his breast.

It was but the next month, I think, that the village lawyer stood reading aloud the account of the capture of a great Sepoy fort. The veteran entered the post-office, and all made way for him. The reading went on:—

"The blowing open of the Northern Gate was the grandest personal exploit of the attack. It was performed by native sappers, covered by the fire of two regiments, and headed by Lieutenants Holder and Dacre, Sergeants Green, Carmody, Macpherson, and Locke."

The lawyer paused. Every eye turned to the face of the old Waterloo soldier. He straightened up to keener attention, threw out his chest, and tapped the glorious medal in salute of the names of the brave.

"God be praised, my son was there!" he said. "Read on."

"Sergeant Carmody, while laying the powder, was killed, and the native havildar wounded. The powder having been laid, the advance party slipped down into the ditch to allow the firing party, under Lieutenant Dacre, to do its duty. While trying to fire the charge he was shot through one arm and leg. He sank, but handed the match to Sergeant Macpherson, who was at once shot dead. Sergeant Locke, already wounded severely in the shoulder, then seized the match, and succeeded in firing the train. He fell at that moment, literally riddled with bullets."

"Read on," said old John, in a deeper voice. All forbore to look twice upon his face.

"Others of the party were falling, when the mighty gate was blown to fragments, and the waiting regiments of infantry, under Colonel Campbell, rushed into the breach."

There was a long silence in the post-office, till old John spoke once more.

"The Lord God be thanked for all his dealings with us! My son, Sergeant Locke, died well for England, Queen, and Duty."

Nervously fingering the treasure on his breast, the old soldier wheeled about, and marched proudly straight down the middle of the village street to his lonely cabin.

The villagers never saw him in life again. Next day he did not appear. All refrained from intruding on his mourning. But in the evening, when the Anglican minister heard of his parishioner's loss, he walked to old John's home.

There, stretched upon his straw bed, he lay in his antique regimentals, stiffer than At Attention, all his medals fastened below that of Waterloo above his quiet heart. His right hand lay on an open Bible, and his face wore an expression as of looking for ever and ever upon Sergeant Locke and the Great Commander who takes back unto Him the heroes He fashions to sweeten the world.

The Ride By Night

Mr. Adam Baines is a little gray about the temples, but still looks so young that few could suppose him to have been one of the fifty-three thousand Canadians who served Abraham Lincoln's cause in the Civil War. Indeed, he was in the army less than a year. How he went out of it he told me in some such words as these:—

An orderly from the direction of Meade's headquarters galloped into our parade ground, and straight for the man on guard before the colonel's tent. That was pretty late in the afternoon of a bright March day in 1865, but the parade ground was all red mud with shallow pools. I remember well how the hind hoofs of the orderly's galloper threw away great chunks of earth as he splashed diagonally across the open.

His rider never slowed till he brought his horse to its haunches before the sentry. There he flung himself off instantly, caught up his sabre, and ran through the middle opening of the high screen of sapling pines stuck on end, side by side, all around the acre or so occupied by the officers' quarters.

The day, though sunny, was not warm, and nearly all the men of my regiment were in their huts when that galloping was heard. Then they hurried out like bees from rows of hives, ran up the lanes between the lines of huts, and collected, each company separately, on the edge of the parade ground opposite the officers' quarters.

You see we had a notion that the orderly had brought the word to break camp. For five months the Army of the Potomac had been in winter quarters, and for weeks nothing more exciting than vidette duty had broken the monotony of our brigade. We understood that Sheridan had received command of all Grant's cavalry, but did not know but the orderly had rushed from Sheridan himself. Yet we awaited the man's re-appearance with intense curiosity.

Soon, instead of the orderly, out ran our first lieutenant, a small, wiry, long-haired man named Miller. He was in undress uniform,— just a blouse and trousers,—and bare-headed. Though he wore low shoes, he dashed through mud and water toward us, plainly in a great hurry.

"Sergeant Kennedy, I want ten men at once—mounted," Miller said. "Choose the ten best able for a long ride, and give them the best horses in the company. You understand,—no matter whose the ten best horses are, give 'em to the ten best riders."

"I understand, sir," said Kennedy.

By this time half the company had started for the stables, for fully half considered themselves among the best riders. The lieutenant laughed at their eagerness.

"Halt, boys!" he cried. "Sergeant, I'll pick out four myself. Come yourself, and bring Corporal Crowfoot, Private Bader, and Private Absalom Gray."

Crowfoot, Bader, and Gray had been running for the stables with the rest. Now these three old soldiers grinned and walked, as much as to say, "We needn't hurry; we're picked anyhow;" while the others hurried on. I remained near Kennedy, for I was so young and green a soldier that I supposed I had no chance to go.

"Hurry up! parade as soon as possible. One day's rations; light marching order—no blankets—fetch over-coats and ponchos," said Miller, turning; "and in choosing your men, favor light weights."

That was, no doubt, the remark which brought me in. I was lanky, light, bred among horses, and one of the best in the regiment had fallen to my lot. Kennedy wheeled, and his eye fell on me.

"Saddle up, Adam, boy," said he; "I guess you'll do."

Lieutenant Miller ran back to his quarters, his long hair flying wide. When he reappeared fifteen minutes later, we were trotting across the parade ground to meet him. He was mounted, not on his own charger, but on the colonel's famous thorough-bred bay. Then we knew a hard ride must be in prospect.

"What! one of the boys?" cried Miller, as he saw me. "He's too young."

"He's very light, sir; tough as hickory. I guess he'll do," said Kennedy.

"Well, no time to change now. Follow me! But, hang it, you've got your carbines! Oh, I forgot! Keep pistols only! throw down your sabres and carbines—anywhere—never mind the mud!"

As we still hesitated to throw down our clean guns, he shouted: "Down with them—anywhere! Now, boys, after me, by twos! Trot—gallop!"

Away we went, not a man jack of us knew for where or what. The colonel and officers, standing grouped before regimental headquarters, volleyed a cheer at us. It was taken up by the whole regiment; it was taken up by the brigade; it was repeated by regiment after regiment of infantry as we galloped through the great camp toward the left front of the army. The speed at which Miller led over a rough corduroy road was extraordinary, and all the men suspected some desperate enterprise afoot.

Red and brazen was the set of the sun. I remember it well, after we got clear of the forts, clear of the breastworks, clear of the reserves, down the long slope and across the wide ford of Grimthorpe's Creek, never drawing rein.

The lieutenant led by ten yards or so. He had ordered each two to take as much distance from the other two in advance; but we rode so fast that the water from the heels of his horse and from the heels of each two splashed into the faces of the following men.

From the ford we loped up a hill, and passed the most advanced infantry pickets, who laughed and chaffed us, asking us for locks of our hair, and if our mothers knew we were out, and promising to report our last words faithfully to the folks at home.

Soon we turned to the left again, swept close by several cavalry videttes, and knew then that we were bound for a ride through a country that might or might not be within Lee's outer lines, at that time extended so thinly in many places that his pickets were far out of touch with one another. To this day I do not know precisely where we went, nor precisely what for. Soldiers are seldom informed of the meaning of their movements.

What I do know is what we did while I was in the ride. As we were approaching dense pine woods the lieutenant turned in his saddle, slacked pace a little, and shouted, "Boys, bunch up near me!"

He screwed round in his saddle so far that we could all see and hear, and said:—

"Boys, the order is to follow this road as fast as we can till our horses drop, or else the Johnnies drop us, or else we drop upon three brigades of our own infantry. I guess they've got astray somehow; but I don't know myself what the trouble is. Our orders are plain. The brigades are supposed to be somewhere on this road. I guess we shall do a big thing if we reach those men to-night. All we've got to do is to ride and deliver this despatch to the general in command. You all understand?"

"Yes, sir! Yes, sir! Yes, sir!"

"It's necessary you all should. Hark, now! We are not likely to strike the enemy in force, but we are likely to run up against small parties. Now, Kennedy, if they down me, you are to stop just long enought to grab the despatch from my breast; then away you go, —always on the main road. If they down you after you've got the paper, the man who can grab it first is to take it and hurry forward. So on right to the last man. If they down him, and he's got his senses when he falls, he's to tear the paper up, and scatter it as widely as he can. You all understand?"

"Yes, sir! Yes, sir!"

"All right, then. String out again!"

He touched the big bay with the spur, and shot quickly ahead.

With the long rest of the winter our horses were in prime spirits, though mostly a little too fleshy for perfect condition. I had cared well for my horse; he was fast and sound in wind and limb. I was certainly the lightest rider of the eleven.

I was still thinking of the probability that I should get further on the way than any comrade except the lieutenant, or perhaps Crowfoot and Bader, whose horses were in great shape; I was thinking myself likely to win promotion before morning, when a cry came out of the darkness ahead. The words of the challenge I was not able to catch, but I heard Miller shout, "Forward, boys!"

We shook out more speed just as a rifle spat its long flash at us from about a hundred yards ahead. For one moment I plainly saw the Southerner's figure. Kennedy reeled beside me, flung up his hands with a scream, and fell. His horse stopped at once. In a moment the lieutenant had ridden the sentry down.

Then from the right side of the road a party, who must have been lying round the camp-fire that we faintly saw in among the pines, let fly at us. They had surely been surprised in their sleep. I clearly saw them as their guns flashed.

"Forward! Don't shoot! Ride on," shouted Miller. "Bushwhackers! Thank God, not mounted! Any of you make out horses with them?"

"No, sir! No, sir!"

"Who yelled? who went down?"

"Kennedy, sir," I cried.

"Too bad! Any one else?"

"No, sir."

"All safe?"

"I'm touched in my right arm; but it's nothing." I said. The twinge was slight, and in the fleshy place in front of my shoulder. I could not make out that I was losing blood, and the pain from the hurt was scarcely perceptible.

"Good boy! Keep up, Adam!" called the lieutenant with a kind tone. I remember my delight that he spoke my front name. On we flew.

Possibly the shots had been heard by the party half a mile further on, for they greeted us with a volley. A horse coughed hard and pitched down behind me. His rider yelled as he fell. Then two more shots came: Crowfoot reeled in front of me, and somehow checked his horse. I saw him no more. Next moment we were upon the group with our pistols.

"Forward, men! Don't stop to fight!" roared Miller, as he got clear. A rifle was fired so close to my head that the flame burned my back hair, and my ears rang for half an hour or more. My bay leaped high and dashed down a man. In a few seconds I was fairly out of the scrimmage.

How many of my comrades had gone down I knew not, nor beside whom I was riding. Suddenly our horses plunged into a hole; his stumbled, the man pitched forward, and was left behind. Then I heard a shot, the clatter of another falling horse, the angry yell of another thrown rider.

On we went,—the relics of us. Now we rushed out of the pine forest into broad moonlight, and I saw two riders between me and the lieutenant,—one man almost at my shoulder, and another galloping ten yards behind. Very gradually this man dropped to the rear. We had lost five men already, and still the night was young.

Bader and Absalom Gray were nearest me. Neither spoke a word till we struck upon a space of sandy road. Then I could hear, far behind the rear man, a sound of galloping on the hard highway.

"They're after us, lieutenant!" shouted Bader.

"Many?" He slacked speed, and we listened attentively.

"Only one," cried Miller. "He's coming fast."

The pursuer gained so rapidly that we looked to our pistols again. Then Absalom Gray cried:

"It's only a horse!"

In a few moments the great gray of fallen Corporal Crowfoot overtook us, went ahead, and slacked speed by the lieutenant.

"Good! He'll be fresh when the rest go down!" shouted Miller. "Let the last man mount the gray!"

By this time we had begun to think ourselves clear of the enemy, and doomed to race on till the horses should fall.

Suddenly the hoofs of Crowfoot's gray and the lieutenant's bay thundered upon a plank road whose hollow noise, when we all reached it, should have been heard far. It took us through wide orchard lands into a low-lying mist by the banks of a great marsh, till we passed through that fog, strode heavily up a slope, and saw the shimmer of roofs under the moon. Straight through the main street we pounded along.

Whether it was wholly deserted I know not, but not a human being was in the streets, nor any face visible at the black windows. Not even a dog barked. I noticed no living thing except some turkeys roosting on a fence, and a white cat that sprang upon the pillar of a gateway and thence to a tree.

Some of the houses seemed to have been ruined by a cannonade. I suppose it was one of the places almost destroyed in Willoughby's recent raid. Here we thundered, expecting ambush and conflict every moment, while the loneliness of the street imposed on me such a sense as might come of galloping through a long cemetery of the dead.

Out of the village we went off the planks again upon sand. I began to suspect that I was losing a good deal of blood. My brain was on fire with whirling thoughts and wonder where all was to end. Out of this daze I came, in amazement to find that we were quickly overtaking our lieutenant's thorough-bred.

Had he been hit in the fray, and bled to weakness? I only know that, still galloping while we gained, the famous horse lurched forward, almost turned a somersault, and fell on his rider.

"Stop—the paper!" shouted Bader.

We drew rein, turned, dismounted, and found Miller's left leg under the big bay's shoulder. The horse was quite dead, the rider's long hair lay on the sand, his face was white under the moon!

We stopped long enough to extricate him, and he came to his senses just as we made out that his left leg was broken.

"Forward!" he groaned. "What in thunder are you stopped for? Oh, the despatch! Here! away you go! Good-bye."

In attending to Miller we had forgotten the rider who had been long gradually dropping behind. Now as we galloped away,—Bader, Absalom Gray, myself, and Crowfoot's riderless horse,—I looked behind for that comrade; but he was not to be seen or heard. We three were left of the eleven.

From the loss of so many comrades the importance of our mission seemed huge. With the speed, the noise, the deaths, the strangeness of the gallop through that forsaken village, the wonder how all would end, the increasing belief that thousands of lives depended on our success, and the longing to win, my brain was wild. A raging desire to be first held me, and I galloped as if in a dream.

Bader led; the riderless gray thundered beside him; Absalom rode stirrup to stirrup with me. He was a veteran of the whole war. Where it was that his sorrel rolled over I do not remember at all, though I perfectly remember how Absalom sprang up, staggered, shouted, "My foot is sprained!" and fell as I turned to look at him and went racing on.

Then I heard above the sound of our hoofs the voice of the veteran of the war. Down as he was, his spirit was unbroken. In the favorite song of the army his voice rose clear and gay and piercing:—

> "Hurrah for the Union!
> Hurrah, boys, hurrah!
> Shouting the battle-cry of freedom!"

We turned our heads and cheered him as we flew, for there was something indescribably inspiring in the gallant and cheerful lilt of the fallen man. It was as if he flung us, from the grief of utter defeat, a soul unconquerable; and I felt the life in me strengthened by the tone.

Old Bader and I for it! He led by a hundred yards, and Crowfoot's gray kept his stride. Was I gaining on them? How was it that I could see his figure outlined more clearly against the horizon? Surely dawn was not coming on!

No; I looked round on a world of naked peach-orchards, and corn-fields ragged with last year's stalks, all dimly lit by a moon that showed far from midnight; and that faint light on the horizon was not in the east, but in the west. The truth flashed on me,—I was looking at such an illumination of the sky as would be caused by the camp-fires of an army.

"The missing brigade!" I shouted.

"Or a Southern division!" Bader cried. "Come on!"

"Come on!" I was certainly gaining on him, but very slowly. Before the nose of my bay was beyond the tail of his roan, the wide illuminations had become more distinct; and still not a vidette, not a picket, not a sound of the proximity of an army.

Bader and I now rode side by side, and Crowfoot's gray easily kept the pace. My horse was in plain distress, but Bader's was nearly done.

"Take the paper, Adam," he said; "my roan won't go much further. Good-bye, youngster. Away you go!" and I drew now quickly ahead.

Still Bader rode on behind me. In a few minutes he was consider-ably behind. Perhaps the sense of being alone increased my feeling of weakness. Was I going to reel out of the saddle? Had I lost so much blood as that? Still I could hear Bader riding on. I turned to look at him. Already he was scarcely visible. Soon he dropped out of sight; but still I heard the laborious pounding of his desperate horse.

My bay was gasping horribly. How far was that faintly yellow sky ahead? It might be two, it might be five miles. Were Union or Southern soldiers beneath it? Could it be conceived that no troops of the enemy were between me and it?

Never mind; my orders were clear. I rode straight on, and I was still riding straight on, marking no increase in the distress of my bay, when he stopped as if shot, staggered, fell on his knees, tried to rise, rolled to his side, groaned and lay.

I was so weak I could not clear myself. I remember my right spur catching in my saddlecloth as I tried to free my foot; then I pitched forward and fell. Not yet senseless, I clutched at my breast for the despatch, meaning to tear it to pieces; but there my brain failed, and in full view of the goal of the night I lay unconscious.

When I came to, I rose on my left elbow, and looked around. Near my feet my poor bay lay, stone dead. Crowfoot's gray!—where was Crowfoot's gray? It flashed on me that I might mount the fresh horse and ride on. But where was the gray? As I peered round I heard faintly the sound of a galloper. Was he coming my way? No; faintly and more faintly I heard the hoofs.

Had the gray gone on then, without the despatch? I clutched at my breast. My coat was unbuttoned—the paper was gone!

Well, sir, I cheered. My God! but it was comforting to hear those far-away hoofs, and know that Bader must have come up, taken the papers, and mounted Crowfoot's gray, still good for a ten-mile ride! The despatch was gone forward; we had not all fallen in vain; maybe the brigades would be saved!

How purely the stars shone! When I stifled my groaning they seemed to tell me of a great peace to come. How still was the night! and I thought of the silence of the multitudes who had died for the Union.

Now the galloping had quite died away. There was not a sound,— a slight breeze blew, but there were no leaves to rustle. I put my head down on the neck of my dead horse. Extreme fatigue was benumbing the pain of my now swelling arm; perhaps sleep was near, perhaps I was swooning.

But a sound came that somewhat revived me. Far, low, joyful, it crept on the air. I sat up, wide awake. The sound, at first faint, died as the little breeze fell, then grew in the lull, and came ever more clearly as the wind arose. It was a sound never to be forgotten,—the sound of the distant cheering of thousands of men.

Then I knew that Bader had galloped into the Union lines, delivered the despatch, and told a story which had quickly passed through wakeful brigades.

Bader I never saw again, nor Lieutenant Miller, nor any man with whom I rode that night. When I came to my senses I was in hospital at City Point. Thence I went home invalided. No surgeon, no nurse, no soldier at the hospital could tell me of my regiment, or how or why I was where I was. All they could tell me was that Richmond was taken, the army far away in pursuit of Lee, and a rumor flying that the great commander of the South had surrendered near Appomattox Court House.

"Drafted"

Harry Wallbridge, awaking with a sense of some alarming sound, listened intently in the darkness, seeing overhead the canvas roof faintly outlined, the darker stretch of its ridgepole, its two thin slanting rafters, and the gable ends of the winter hut. He could not hear small, fine drizzle from an atmosphere sur-charged with water, nor anything but the drip from canvas to trench, the rustling of hay bunched beneath his head, the regular breathing of his "buddy," Corporal Bader, and the stamping of horses in stables. But when a soldier in a neighboring tent called indistinguishably in the accents of nightmare, Bader's breathing quieted, and in the lull Harry fancied the soaked air weighted faintly with steady picket-firing. A month with the 53d Pennsylvania Veteran Volunteer Cavalry had not quite disabused the young recruit of his schoolboy belief that the men of the Army of the Potomac must live constantly within sound of the out-posts.

Harry sat up to hearken better, and then concluded that he had mistaken for musketry the crackle of haystalks under his poncho sheet. Beneath him the round poles of his bed sagged as he drew up his knees and gathered about his shoulders the gray blanket damp from the spray of heavy rain against the canvas earlier in the night. Soon, with slow dawn's approach, he could make out the dull white of his carbine and sabre against the mud-plastered chimney. In that drear dimness the boy shivered, with a sense of misery rather than from cold, and yearned as only sleepy youth can for the ease of a true bed and dry warm swooning to slumber. He was sustained by no mature sense that this too would pass; it was with a certain bodily despair that he felt chafed and compressed by his rough garments, and pitied himself, thinking how his mother would cry if she could see him couched so wretchedly that wet March morning, pressed all the more into loneliness by the regular breathing of veteran Bader in the indifference of deep sleep.

Harry's vision of his mother coming into his room, shading her candle with her hand, to see if he were asleep, passed away as a small gust came, shaking the canvas, for he was instantly alert with a certainty that the breeze had borne a strong rolling of musketry.

"Bader, Bader!" he said. "Bader!"

"Can't you shut up, you Wallbridge?" came Orderly Sergeant Gravely's sharp tones from the next tent.

"What's wrong with you, Harry, boy?" asked Bader, turning.

"I thought I heard heavy firing closer than the picket lines; twice now I've thought I heard it."

"Oh, I guess not, Harry. The Johnnies won't come out no such night as this. Keep quiet, or you'll have the sergeant on top of you. Better lie down and try to sleep, buddy; the bugles will call morning soon now."

Again Harry fell to his revery of home, and his vision became that of the special evening on which his boyish wish to go to war had, for the family's sake, become resolve. He saw his mother's spectacled and lamp-lit face as she, leaning to the table, read in the familiar Bible; little Fred and Mary, also facing the table's central lamp, bent sleepy heads over their school-books; the father sat in the rocking-chair, with his right hand on the paper he had laid down, and gazed gloomily at the coals fallen below the front doors of the wood-burning stove. Harry dreamed himself back in his own chair, looking askance, and feeling sure his father was inwardly groaning over the absence of Jack, the eldest son. Then nine o'clock struck, and Fred and Mary began to put their books away in preparation for bed.

"Wait a little, children," Mrs. Wallbridge said, serene in tone from her devotional reading. "Father wants that I should tell you something. You mustn't feel bad about it. It's that we may soon go out West. Your Uncle Ezra is doing well in Minnesota. Aunt Elvira says so in her letter that came to-day."

"It's this way, children," said Mr. Wallbridge, ready to explain, now that the subject was opened. "Since ever your brother Jack went away South, the store expenses have been too heavy. It's near five years now he's been gone. There's a sheaf of notes coming due the third of next month; twice they've been renewed, and the Philadelphia men say they'll close me up this time sure. If I had eight hundred dollars— but it's no use talking; we'll just have to let them take what we've got. Times have been bad right along around here, anyhow, with new competition, and so many farmers gone to the war, and more gone West. If Jack had stopped to home—but I've had to pay two clerks to do his work, and then they don't take any interest in the business. Mind, I'm not blaming Jack, poor fellow,—he'd a right to go where he'd get more'n his keep, and be able to lay up something for himself,—but what's become of him, God knows; and such a smart, good boy as he was! He'd got fond of New Orleans,—I guess some nice girl there, maybe, was the reason; and there he'd stay after the war began, and now it's two years and more since we've heard from him. Dead, maybe, or maybe they'd put him in jail, for he said he'd never join the Confeder-ates, nor fight against them either—he felt that way—North and South was all the same to him. And so he's gone; and I don't see my way now at all. Ma, if it wasn't for my lame leg, I'd take the bounty. It'd be *something* for you and the children after the store's gone."

"Sho, pa! don't talk that way! You're too down-hearted. It'll all come right, with the Lord's help," said Harry's mother. How clearly he, in the damp cold tent, could see her kind looks as she pushed up her spectacles and beamed on her husband; how distinctly, in the still dim dawn, he heard her soothing tones!

It was that evening's talk which had sent Harry, so young, to the front. Three village boys, little older than he, had already contrived to enlist. Every time he saw the Flag drooping, he thought shame of him-self to be absent from the ranks of its upholders; and now, just as he was believing himself big and old enough to serve, he conceived that duty to his parents distinctly enjoined him to go. So in the night, without leave-taking or consent of his parents, he departed. The combined Federal, State, and city bounties offered at Philadelphia amounted to nine hundred dollars cash that dreadful winter before Richmond fell, and Harry sent the money home triumphantly in time to pay his father's notes and save the store.

While the young soldier thought it all over, carbine and sabre came out more and more distinctly outlined above the mud-plastered fireplace. The drizzle had ceased, the drip into the trench was almost finished, intense stillness ruled; Harry half expected to hear cocks crow from out such silence.

Listening for them, his dreamy mind brooded over both hosts, in a vision even as wide as the vast spread of the Republic in which they lay as two huddles of miserable men. For what were they all about him this woful, wet night? they all fain, as he, for home and industry and comfort. What delusion held them? How could it be that they could not all march away and separate, and the cruel war be over? Harry caught his breath at the idea,—it seemed so natural, simple, easy, and good a solution. Becoming absorbed in the fancy, tired of listening, and soothed by the silence, he was falling asleep as he sat, when a heavy weight seemed to fall, far away. Another—another—the fourth had the rumble of distant thunder, and seemed followed by a concussion of the air.

"Hey—Big Guns! What's up toward City Point?" cried Bader, sitting up. "I tell you they're at it. It can't be so far away as Butler. What? On the left too! That was toward Hatcher's Run! Harry, the rebs are out in earnest! I guess you did hear the pickets trying to stop 'em. What a morning! Ha—Fort Hell! see that!"

The outside world was dimly lighted up for a moment. In the intensified darkness that followed Bader's voice was drowned by the crash of a great gun from the neighboring fort. *Flash, crash—flash, crash—flash, crash* succeeded rapidly. Then the intervals of Fort Hell's fire lengthened to the regular periods for loading, and between her roars were heard the sullen boom of more distant guns, while through all the tumult ran a fierce undertone,—the infernal hurrying of musketry along the immediate front.

"The Johnnies must have got in close somehow," cried Bader. "Hey, Sergeant?"

"Yes," shouted Gravely. "Scooped up the pickets and supports too in the rain, I guess. Turn out, boys, turn out! there'll be a wild day. Kid! Where's the Kid? Kid Sylvester!"

"Here! All right, Barney; I'll be out in two shakes," shouted the bugler.

"Hurry, then! I can hear the Colonel shouting already. Man, listen to that!"—as four of Fort Hell's guns crashed almost simultaneously. "Brownie! Greasy Cook! O Brownie!"

"Here!" shouted the cook.

"Get your fire started right away, and see what salt horse and biscuit you can scare up. Maybe we'll have time for a snack."

"Turn out, Company K!" shouted Lieutenant Bradley, running down from the officers' quarters. "Where's the commissary sergeant? There?—all right—give out feed right away! Get your oats, men, and feed instantly. We may have time. Hullo! here's the General's orderly."

As the trooper galloped, in a mud-storm, across the parade ground, a group of officers ran out behind the Colonel from the screen of pine saplings about Regimental Headquarters. The orderly gave the Colonel but a word, and, wheeling, was off again as "Boot and saddle" blared from the buglers, who had now assembled on parade.

"But leave the bits out—let your horses feed!" cried the Lieutenant, running down again. "We're not to march till further orders."

Beyond the screen of pines Harry could see the tall canvas ridges of the officers' cabins lighted up. Now all the tents of the regiment, row behind row, were faintly luminous, and the renewed drizzle of the dawn was a little lightened in every direction by the canvas-hidden candles of infantry regiments, the glare of numerous fires already started, and sparks showering up from the cook-houses of company after company.

Soon in the cloudy sky the cannonade rolled about in broad day, which was still so gray that long wide flashes of flame could be seen to spring far out before every report from the guns of Fort Hell, and in the haze but few of the rebel shells shrieking along their high curve could be clearly seen bursting over Hancock's cheering men. Indistinguishably blent were the sounds of hosts on the move, field-guns pounding to the front, troops shouting, the clink and rattle of metal, officers calling, bugles blaring, drums rolling, mules screaming,— all heard as a running accompaniment to the cannon heavily punctuating the multitudinous din.

"Fwat sinse in the ould man bodderin' us?" grumbled Corporal Kennedy, a tall Fenian dragoon from the British army. "Sure, ain't it as plain as the sun—and faith the same's not plain this dirthy mornin' —that there's no work for cavalry the day, barrin' its escortin' the doughboys' prisoners, if they take any?—bad 'cess to the job. Sure it's an infantry fight, and must be, wid the field-guns helpin', and the siege pieces boomin' away over the throops in the mud betwigst our own breastworks and the inner line of our forts." ·

"Oh, by this and by that," the corporal grumbled on, "ould Lee's not the gintleman I tuk him for at all, at all,—discomfortin' us in the rain,—and yesterday an illigant day for fightin'. Couldn't he wait, like the dacint ould boy he's reported, for a dhry mornin', instead av turnin' his byes out in the shlush and destroyin' me chanst av breakfast? It's spring chickens I'd ordhered."

"You may get up to spring-chicken country soon, now," said Bader. "I'm thinking this is near the end; it's the last assault that Lee will ever deliver."

"Faith, I dunno," said the corporal; "that's what we've been saying sinst last fall, but the shtay of them Johnnies bates Banagher and the prophets. Hoo—ow! by the powers! did you hear them yell? Fwat? The saints be wid us! who'd'a'thought it possible? Byes! Bader! Harry! luk at the Johnnies swarmin' up the face of Hell!"

Off there Harry could dimly see, rising over the near horizon made by tents, a straggling rush of men up the steep slope, while the rebel yell came shrill from a multitude behind on the level ground that was hidden from the place occupied by the cavalry regiment. In the next moment the force mounting Fort Hell's slope fell away, some lying where shot down, some rolling, some running and stumbling in heaps; then a tremendous musketry and field-gun fire growled to and fro under the heavy smoke round and about and out in front of the embrasures, which had never ceased their regular discharge over the heads of the fort's defenders and immediate assailants.

Suddenly Harry noted a slackening of the battle; it gradually but soon dropped away to nothing, and now no sound of small-arms in any direction was heard in the lengthening intervals of reports from the siege pieces far and near.

"And so that's the end of it," said Kennedy. "Sure it was hot work for a while! Faix, I thought onct the doughboys was nappin' too long, and ould Hell would be bullyin' away at ourselves. Now, thin, can we have a bite in paice? I'll shtart wid a few sausages, Brownie, and you may send in the sphring chickens wid some oyshters the second coorse. No! Oh, by the powers, 't is too mane to lose a breakfast like that!" and Corporal Kennedy shook his fist at the group of buglers calling the regiment to parade.

In ten minutes the Fifty-third had formed in column of companies. "Old Jimmy," their Colonel, had galloped down at them and once along their front; then the command, forming fours from the right front, moved off at a trot through the mud in long procession.

"Didn't I know it?" said Kennedy; "it's escortin' the doughboys' prisoners, that's all we're good for this outrageous day. Oh, wirra, wirrasthru! Police duty! and this calls itself a cavalry rigiment. Mounted Police duty,—escortin' doughboys' prisoners! Faix, I might as well be wid Her Majesty's dhragoons, thramplin' down the flesh and blood of me in poor ould Oireland. Begor, Harry, me bhy, it's a mane job to be setting you at, and this the first day ye're mounted to save the Union!"

"Stop coddin' the boy, Corporal," said Bader, angrily. "You can't think how an American boy feels about this war."

"An Amerikin!—an Amerikin, is it? Let me insthruct ye thin, Misther Bader, that I'm as good an Amerikin as the next man. Och, be jabers, me that's been in the color you see ever since the Prisident first called for men! It was for a three months' dance he axed us first. Me, that's re-enlishted twice, don't know the feelin's of an Amerikin! What am I here for? Not poverty! sure I'd enough of that before ever I seen Ameriky! What am I wallopin' through the mud for this mornin'?"

"It's your trade, Kennedy," said Bader, with disgust.

"Be damned to you, man!" said the corporal, sternly. "When I touched fut in New York, didn't I swear that I'd never dhraw swoord more, barrin' it was agin the ould red tyrant and oprissor of me counthry? Wasn't I glad to be dhrivin' me own hack next year in Philamedink like a gintleman? Oh, the paice and the indipindence of it! But what cud I do when the counthry that tuk me and was good to me wanted an ould dhragoon? An Amerikin, ye say! Faith, the heart of me is Amerikin, if I'm a bog throtter by the tongue. Mind that now, me bould man!"

Harry heard without heeding as the horses spattered on. Still wavered in his ears the sounds of the dawn; still he saw the ghostlike forms of Americans in gray tumbling back from their rush against the sacred flag that had drooped so sadly over the smoke; and still, far away beyond all this puddled and cumbered ground the dreamy boy saw millions of white American faces, all haggard for news of the armies —some looking South, some North, yearning for the Peace that had so long ago been the boon of the Nation.

Now the regiment was upon the red clay of the dead fight, and brought to halt in open columns. After a little they moved off again in fours, and, dropping into single file, surrounded some thousands of disarmed men, the remnant of the desperate brigades that Lee had flung through the night across three lines of breastworks at the great fort they had so nearly stormed. Poor drenched, shivering Johnnies! there they stood, not a few of them in blue overcoats, but mostly in butternut, generally tattered; some barefoot, some with feet bound in ragged sections of blanket, many with toes and skin showing through crazy boots lashed on with strips of cotton or with cord; many stoutly on foot, streaming blood from head wounds.

Some lay groaning in the mud, while their comrades helped Union surgeons to bind or amputate. Here and there groups huddled together in earnest talk, or listened to comrades gesticulating and storming as they recounted incidents of the long charge. But far the greater number faced outward, at gaze upon the cavalry guard, and, silently munching thick flat cakes of corn-bread, stared into the faces of the horsemen. Harry Wallbridge, brought to the halt, faced half round in the saddle, and looked with quick beatings of pity far and wide over the disorderly crowd of weather-worn men.

"It's a Louisiana brigade," said Bader.

"Fifty-three, P.V.C.," spoke a prisoner, as if in reply, reading the letters about the little crossed brass sabres on the Union hats. "Say, you men from Pennsylvany?"

"Yes, Johnny; we come down to wake up Dixie."

"I reckon we got the start at wakin' you this mornin'," drawled the Southerner. "But say,—there's one of our boys lyin' dyin' over yonder; his folks lived in Pennsylvany. Mebbe some of you 'ud know 'em."

"What's his name?" asked Bader.

"Wallbridge—Johnny Wallbridge."

"Why, Harry—hold on!—you ain't the only Wallbridges there is. What's up?" cried Bader, as the boy half reeled, half clambered from his saddle.

"Hold on, Harry!" cried Corporal Kennedy.

"Halt there, Wallbridge!" shouted Sergeant Gravely.

"Stop that man!" roared Lieutenant Bradley.

But, calling, "He's my brother!" Harry, catching up his sabre as he ran, followed the Southerner, who had instantly divined the situation. The forlorn prisoners made ready way for them, and closing in behind, stretched in solid array about the scene.

"It's not Jack," said the boy; but something in the look of the dying man drew him on to kneel in the mud. "Is it *you,* Jack? Oh, now I know you! Jack, I'm Harry! don't you know me? I'm Harry—your brother Harry."

The Southern soldier stared rigidly at the boy, seeming to grow paler with the recollections that he struggled for.

"What's your name?" he asked very faintly.

"Harry Wallbridge—I'm your brother."

"Harry Wallbridge! Why, I'm *John* Wallbridge. Did you say Harry? *Not Harry!"* he shrieked hoarsely. "No; Harry's only a little fellow!" He paused, and looked meditatively into the boy's eyes. "It's nearly five years I've been gone,—he was near twelve then. Boys," lifting his head painfully and casting his look slowly round upon his comrades, "I know him by the eyes; yes, he's my brother! Let me speak to him alone—stand back a bit," and at once the men pushed backward into the form of a wide circle.

"Put down your head, Harry. Kiss me! Kiss me again!—how's mother? Ah, I was afraid she might be dead—don't tell her I'm dead, Harry." He groaned with the pain of the groin wound. "Closer, Harry; I've got to tell you this first—maybe it's all I've time to tell. Say, Harry," —he began to gasp,—"they didn't ought to have killed me, the Union soldiers didn't. I never fired—high enough—all these years. They drafted me, Harry—tell mother that—down in New Orleans—and I—couldn't get away. Ai—ai! how it hurts! I must die soon's I can tell you. I wanted to come home—and help father—how's poor father, Harry? Doing well now? Oh, I'm glad of that—and the baby? there's a new baby! Ah, yes, I'll never see it, Harry."

His eyes closed, the pain seemed to leave him, and he lay almost smiling happily as his brother's tears fell on his muddy and blood-clotted face. As if from a trance his eyes opened, and he spoke anxiously but calmly.

"You'll be sure to tell them I was drafted—conscripted, you understand. And I never fired at any of us—of you—tell all the boys *that."* Again the flame of life went down, and again flickered up in pain.

"Harry—you'll stay by father—and help him, won't you? This cruel war—is almost over. Don't cry. Kiss me. Say—do you remember—the old times we had—fishing? Kiss me again, Harry—brother in blue—you're on—*my* side. Oh I wish—I had time—to tell you. Come close—put your arms around—my neck—it's old times—again." And now the wound tortured him for a while beyond speech. "You're with me, aren't you, Harry?

"Well, there's this," he gasped on, "about my chums—they've been as good and kind—marching us all wet and cold together—and it wasn't their fault. If they had known—how I wanted—to be shot—for the Union! It was so hard—to be—on the wrong side! But—"

He lifted his head and stared wildly at his brother, screamed rapidly, as if summoning all his life for the effort to explain, "Drafted, *drafted, drafted*—Harry, tell mother and father *that*. I was *drafted*. O God, O God, what suffering! Both sides—I was on both sides all the time. I loved them all, North and South, all,—but the Union most. O God, it was so hard!"

His head fell back, his eyes closed, and Harry thought it was the end. But once more Jack opened his blue eyes, and slowly said in a steady, clear, anxious voice, "Mind you tell them I never fired high enough!" .Then he lay still in Harry's arms, breathing fainter and fainter till no motion was on his lips, nor in his heart, nor any tremor in the hands that lay in the hand of his brother in blue.

"Come, Harry," said Bader, stooping tenderly to the boy, "the order is to march. He's past helping now. It's no use; you must leave him here to God. Come, boy, the head of the column is moving already."

Mounting his horse, Harry looked across to Jack's form. For the first time in two years the famous Louisiana brigade trudged on without their unwilling comrade. There he lay, alone, in the Union lines, under the rain, his marching done, a figure of eternal peace; while Harry, looking backward till he could no longer distinguish his brother from the clay of the field, rode dumbly on and on beside the downcast procession of men in gray.

Miss Minnely's Management

George Renwick substituted "limb" for "leg," "intoxicated" for "drunk," and "undergarment" for "shirt," in "The Converted Ringmaster," a short-story-of-commerce, which he was editing for "The Family Blessing." When he should have eliminated all indecorum it would go to Miss Minnely, who would "elevate the emotional interest." She was sole owner of "The Blessing," active director of each of its multifarious departments. Few starry names rivalled hers in the galaxy of American character-builders.

Unaware of limitations to her versatility, Miss Minnely might have dictated all the literary contents of the magazine, but for her acute perception that other gifted pens should be enlisted. Hence many minor celebrities worshipped her liberal cheques, whilst her more extravagant ones induced British titled personages to assuage the yearning of the American Plain People for some contact with rank.

Renwick wrought his changes sardonically, applying to each line a set of touchstones—"Will it please Mothers?" "Lady schoolteachers?" "Ministers of the Gospel?" "Miss Minnely's Taste?" He had not entirely converted The Ringmaster when his door was gently opened by the Chief Guide to the Family Blessing Building.

Mr. Durley had grown grey under solemn sense of responsibility for impressions which visitors might receive. With him now appeared an unusually numerous party of the usual mothers, spinsters, aged good men, and anxious children who keep watch and ward over "The Blessing's" pages, in devotion to Miss Minnely's standing editorial request that "subscribers will faithfully assist the Editors with advice, encouragement, or reproof." The Mature, with true American gentleness, let the Young assemble nearest the open door. All necks craned toward Renwick. Because Mr. Durley's discourse to so extensive a party was unusually loud, Renwick heard, for the first time, what the Chief Guide was accustomed to murmur at his threshold: "De-ar friends, the gentleman we now have the satisfaction of beholding engaged in a sitting posture at his editorial duties, is Mr. George Hamilton Renwick, an American in every——."

"He *looks* like he might be English," observed a matron.

Mr. Durley took a steady look at Renwick: "He *is* some red complected, Lady, but I guess it's only he is used to out of doors." He resumed his customary drone:—"Mr. Renwick, besides he is American in every fibre of his being, is a first rate general purpose editor, and also a noted authority on yachting, boating, canoeing, rowing, swimming, and every kind of water amusements of a kind calculated to build up character in subscribers. Mr. George Hamilton Renwick's engagement by 'The Family Blessing' exclusively is a recent instance of many evidences that Miss Minnely, the Sole Proprietress, spares no expense in securing talented men of genius who are likewise authorities on every kind of specialty interesting, instructive, and improving to first-class respectable American families. Ladies and gentlemen, and de-ar children, girls, and youths, we will now pass on to Room Number Sixteen, and behold Mr. Caliphas C. Cummins, the celebrated author and authority on Oriental and Scriptural countries. Mr. Cummins is specially noted as the author of 'Bijah's Bicycle in Babylonia,' 'A Girl Genius at Galilee,' and many first-class serials published exclusively in 'The Family Blessing.' He may——"

Mr. Durley softly closed Renwick's door.

The Improving Editor, now secluded, stared wrathfully for some moments. Then he laughed, seized paper, and wrote in capitals:—

"When the editor in this compartment is to be exhibited, please notify him by knocking on this door before opening it. He will then rise from his sitting posture, come forward for inspection, and turn slowly round three times, if a mother, a school teacher, or a minister of the Gospel be among the visiting subscribers."

Renwick strode to his door. While pinning the placard on its outside he overheard the concluding remarks of Mr. Durley on Mr. Cummins, whose room was next in the long corridor: "Likewise talented editor of the Etiquette Department and the Puzzle Department. Mr. Cummins, Sir, seven lady teachers from the State of Maine are now honouring us in this party."

Renwick stood charmed to listen. He heard the noted author clack forward to shake hands all round, meantime explaining in thin, high, affable volubility: "My de-ar friends, you have the good fortune to behold me in the very act of composing my new serial of ten Chapters, for 'The Blessing' exclusively, entitled 'Jehu and Jerusha in Jerusalem,' being the experiences of a strenuous New England brother and sister in the Holy Land, where our Lord innogerated the Christian religion, now, sad to say, under Mohammetan subjection. In this tale I am incorporating largely truthful incidents of my own and blessed wife's last visit to the Holy Places where——"

Renwick slammed his door. He flung his pen in a transport of derision. Rebounding from his desk, it flew through an open window, perhaps to fall on some visitor to "The Blessing's" lawn. He hastened to look down. Nobody was on the gravel path or bench within possible reach of the missile. Renwick, relieved, mused anew on the singularities of the scene.

The vast "Blessing" Building stands amid a city block devoted largely to shaven turf, flower beds, grassed mounds, and gravel paths. It is approached from the street by a broad walk which bifurcates at thirty yards from the "Richardson" entrance, to surround a turfed truncated cone, from which rises a gigantic, severely draped, female figure. It is that bronze of Beneficence which, in the words of the famous New England sculptress, Miss Angela C. Amory Pue, "closely features Miss Martha Minnely in her grand early womanhood." In the extensive arms of the Beneficence a bronze volume so slants that spectators may read on its back, in gilt letters, *"The Family Blessing."* Prettily pranked out in dwarf marginal plants on the turfy cone these words are pyramided: *"Love. Heaven. Beneficence. The Latest Fashions. My Country, 'tis of Thee."*

Not far from the statue slopes a great grassed mound which displays still more conspicuously in "everlastings," *"The Family Blessing. Circulation 1915, 1,976,709. Monthly. Come Unto Me all Ye Weary And Heavily Laden. Two Dollars a Year."*

The scheme ever puzzled Renwick. Had some demure humour thus addressed advertisements as if to the eternal stars? Or did they proceed from a pure simplicity of commercial taste? From this perennial problem he was diverted by sharp rapping at his door. Durley again? But the visitor was Mr. Joram B. Buntstir, veteran among the numerous editors of "The Blessing," yet capable of jocularities. He appeared perturbed.

"Renwick, you are rather fresh here, and I feel so friendly to you that I'd hate to see you get into trouble unwarned. Surely you can't wish Miss Minnely to see *that."*

"What? Oh, the placard! That's for Durley. He must stop exhibiting me."

"Mr. Durley won't understand. Anyway, he couldn't stop without instructions from Miss Minnely. He will take the placard to her for orders. You do not wish to hurt Miss Minnely's feelings, I am sure." Mr. Buntstir closed the door behind him.

"Bah—Miss Minnely's feelings can't be so tender as all that!"

"No, eh? Do you know her so thoroughly?"

"I don't know her at all. I've been here three months without once seeing Miss Minnely. Is she real? Half the time I doubt her existence."

"You get instructions from her regularly."

"I get typewritten notes, usually voluminous, signed 'M. Minnely,' twice a week. But the Business Manager, or Miss Heartly, may dictate them, for all I know."

"Pshaw! Miss Minnely presides in seclusion. Her private office has a street entrance. She seldom visits the Departments in office hours. Few of her staff know her by sight. She saves time by avoiding personal interviews. But she keeps posted on everybody's work. I hope you may not have to regret learning how very real Miss Minnely can be. She took me in hand, once, eight years ago. I have been careful to incur no more discipline since—kind as she was. If she sees your placard—"

"Well, what?"

"Well, she can be very impressive. I fear your offer to turn round before visitors may bring you trouble."

"I am looking for trouble. I'm sick and tired of this life of intellectual shame."

"Then quit!" snapped Buntstir, pierced. "Be consistent. Get out. Sell your sneers at a great established publication to some pamphlet periodical started by college boys for the regeneration of Literature. Don't jeer what you live by. That is where intellectual shame should come in."

"You are right. A man should not gibe his job. I must quit. The 'Blessing' is all right for convinced devotees of the mawkish. But if a man thinks sardonically of his daily work, that damns the soul."

"It may be an effect of the soul trying to save itself," said Buntstir, mollified, "Anyway, Renwick, remember your trouble with 'The Reflex.' Avoid the name of a confirmed quitter. Stay here till you can change to your profit. Squealing won't do us any good. A little grain of literary conscience ought not to make you *talk* sour. It's cynical to satirize our bread and butter—imprudent, too."

"That's right. I'll swear off, or clear out. Lord, how I wish I could. My brain must rot if I don't. 'The Blessing's' 'emotional'! Oh, Buntstir, the stream of drivel! And to live by concocting it for trustful subscribers. Talk of the sin of paregoricking babies!"

"Babies take paregoric because they like it. Pshaw, Renwick, you're absurdly sensitive. Writing-men must live, somehow—usually by wishy-washiness. Unpleasant work is the common lot of mankind. Where's *your* title to exemption? Really, you're lucky. Miss Minnely perceives zest in your improvements of copy. She says you are naturally gifted with 'The Blessing's' taste."

"For Heaven's sake, Buntstir!"

"She did—Miss Heartly told me so. And yet—if she sees that placard —no one can ever guess what she may do in discipline. You can't wish to be bounced, dear boy, with your family to provide for. Come, you've blown off steam. Take the placard off your door."

"All right. I will. But Miss Minnely can't bounce me without a year's notice. That's how I engaged."

"A year's notice to quit a life of intellectual shame!"

"Well, it is one thing to jump out of the window, and another to be bounced. I wouldn't stand that."

Buntstir laughed. "I fancy I see you, you sensitive Cuss, holding on, or jumping off or doing anything contra to Miss Minnely's intention." He went to the door. "Hello, where's the placard?" he cried, opening it.

"Gone!" Renwick sprang up.

"Gone, sure. No matter how. It is already in Miss Minnely's hands. Well, I told you to take it down twenty minutes ago."

"Wait, Buntstir. What is best to be done?"

"Hang on for developments—and get to work."

Buntstir vanished as one hastens to avoid infection.

II

Renwick resumed his editing of "The Converted Ringmaster" with resolve to think on nothing else. But, between his eyes and the manuscript, came the woeful aspect of two widows, his mother and his sister, as they had looked six months earlier, when he threw up his political editorship of "The Daily Reflex" in disgust at its General Manager's sudden reversal of policy. His sister's baby toddled into the vision. He had scarcely endured to watch the child's uncertain steps during the weeks while he wondered how to buy its next month's modified milk. To "The Reflex" he could not return, because he had publicly burned his boats, with the desperate valour of virtue conscious that it may weaken if strained by need for family food.

Out of that dangerous hole he had been lifted by the Sole Proprietress of "The Family Blessing." She praised his "public stand for principle" in a note marked "strictly confidential," which tendered him a "position." He had secretly laughed at the cautious, amiable offer, even while her laudation gratified his self-importance. Could work on "The Blessing" seem otherwise than ridiculous for one accustomed to chide presidents, monarchs, bosses, bankers, railway magnates? But it was well paid, and seemed only too easy. The young man did not foresee for himself that benumbing of faculty which ever punishes the writer who sells his facility to tasks below his ambition. At worst "The Blessing" seemed harmless. Nor could his better nature deny a certain esteem to that periodical which affectionate multitudes proclaimed to be justly named.

Renwick, viewing himself once more as a recreant breadwinner, cursed his impetuous humour. But again he took heart from remembrance of his engagement by the year, little suspecting his impotency to hold on where snubs must be the portion of the unwanted. Twelve months to turn round in! But after? What if an editor, already reputed impractical by "The Reflex" party, should be refused employment everywhere, after forsaking "The Blessing" office, in which "positions" were notoriously sought or coveted by hundreds of "literary" aspirants to "soft snaps"? So his veering imagination whirled round that inferno into which wage earners descend after hazarding their livelihood.

From this disquiet he sprang when his door was emphatically knocked. It opened. Mr. Durley reappeared with a throng closely resembling the last, except for one notable wide lady in street costume of Quakerish gray. Her countenance seemed to Renwick vaguely familiar. The fabric and cut of her plain garb betokened nothing of wealth to the masculine eye, but were regarded with a degree of awe by the other ladies present. She appeared utterly American, yet unworldly, in the sense of seeming neither citified, suburbanish, nor rural. The experienced placidity of her countenance reminded Renwick of a familiar composite photograph of many matrons chosen from among "The Blessing's" subscribers.

"Her peculiarity is that of the perfect type," he pondered while listening to Durley's repetition of his previous remarks.

At their close, he briskly said: "Mr. Renwick, Sir, Miss Minnely wishes you to know that your kind offer is approved. We are now favoured with the presence of four mothers, six lady teachers, and a minister of the Gospel."

Renwick flushed. His placard approved! It promised that he would come forward and turn round thrice for inspection. Durley had received instructions to take him at his word! Suddenly the dilemma touched his facile humour. Explanation before so many was impossible. Gravely he approached the visitors; held out the skirts of his sack coat, turned slowly thrice, and bowed low at the close.

The large lady nodded with some reserve. Other spectators clearly regarded the solemnity as part of "The Blessing's" routine. Mr. Durley resumed his professional drone:—"We will now pass on to Room Number Sixteen, and behold Mr. Caliphas C. Cummins in——" Renwick's door closed.

Then the large lady, ignoring the attractions of Mr. Cummins, went to the waiting elevator, and said "down."

Renwick, again at his desk, tried vainly to remember of what or whom the placid lady had reminded him. A suspicion that she might be Miss Minnely fled before recollection of her street costume. Still —she *might* be. If so— had his solemnly derisive posturing offended her? She had given no sign. How could he explain his placard to her? Could he not truly allege objections to delay of his work by Durley's frequent interruptions? He was whirling with conjecture and indecision when four measured ticks from a lead pencil came on his outer door.

There stood Miss Heartly, Acting Manager of the Paper Patterns Department. Her light blue eyes beamed the confidence of one born trustful, and confirmd in the disposition by thirty-five years of popularity at home, in church, in office. In stiff white collar, lilac tie, trig grey gown, and faint, fading bloom of countenance, she well represented a notable latter day American type, the Priestess of Business, one born and bred as if to endow office existence with some almost domestic touch of Puritan nicety. That no man might sanely hope to disengage Miss Heartly from devotion to "The Family Blessing" was as if revealed by her unswerving directness of gaze in speech.

"I have called, Mr. Renwick, by instruction of the Sole Proprietress. Miss Minnely wishes me, first, to thank you for this."

It was the placard!

Renwick stared, unable to credit the sincerity in her face and tone. She *must* be making game of him while she spoke in measured links, as if conscientiously repeating bits each separately memorized:

"Mr. Renwick—Miss Minnely desires you to know that she has been rarely more gratified—than by this evidence—that your self-identification with 'The Blessing'—is cordial and complete. But—Miss Minnely is inclined to hope—that your thoughtful and kind proposal— of turning round for inspection—may be—modified—or improved. For instance—if you would carefully prepare—of course for revision by her own taste—a short and eloquent welcoming discourse—to visitors—that could be elevated to an attraction—for subscribers—of that she is almost, though not yet quite, fully assured. Miss Minnely presumes, Mr. Renwick, that you have had the pleasure of—hearing Mr. Cummins welcome visitors. Of course, Mr. Renwick, Miss Minnely would not have *asked* you—but—as you have volunteered—in your cordial willingness—*that* affords her an opportunity—for the suggestion. But, Mr. Renwick, if you do not *like* the idea—then Miss Minnely would not wish—to pursue the suggestion further." A child glad to have repeated its lesson correctly could not have looked more ingenuous.

In her fair countenance, open as a daybook, Renwick could detect no guile. Her tone and figure suggested curiously some flatness, as of the Paper Patterns of her Department. But through this mild deputy Miss Minnely must, he conceived, be deriding him. With what subtlety the messenger had been chosen! It seemed at once necessary and impossible to explain his placard to one so guiltless of humour.

"I hoped it might be understood that I did not intend that placard to be taken literally, Miss Heartly."

"Not literally!" she seemed bewildered.

"To be pointed at as 'a first class general purpose editor' is rather too much, don't you think?"

"I know, Mr. Renwick," she spoke sympathetically. "It sort of got onto your humility, I presume. But Miss Minnely thinks you *are* first class, or she would never have instructed Mr. Durley to *say* first class. That is cordial to you, and good business—to impress the visitors, I mean."

"Miss Minnely is very appreciative and kind. But the point is that I did not engage to be exhibited to flocks of gobemouches."

Miss Heartly pondered the term. "Please, Mr. Renwick, what are gobemouches."

"I should have said The Plain People."

"Perhaps there have been rude ones—not subscribers," she said anxiously.

"No, all have acted as if reared on 'The Blessing.' "

She sighed in relief—then exclaimed in consternation:—"Can Mr. Durley have been—*rude?*" She hesitated to pronounce the dire word.

"Not at all, Miss Heartly. I do not blame Mr. Durley for exhibiting us as gorillas."

"But how *wrong.*" There was dismay in her tone. "Miss Minnely has warned him against the least bit of deception."

"Oh, please, Miss Heartly—I was speaking figuratively."

Her fair brow slightly wrinkled, her fingers went nervously to her anxious lips, she looked perplexed;—"Figuratively! If you would kindly explain, Mr. Renwick. I am not very literary."

"Do the ladies of the Paper Patterns Department *like* to be exhibited?" he ventured.

"Well, I could not exactly be warranted to say 'like'—Scripture has such warnings against the sinfulness of vanity. But we are, of course, cordially pleased to see visitors—it is so good for the Subscription Department."

"I see. And it is not hard on you individually. There you are, a great roomful of beautiful, dutiful, cordial young ladies. You keep one another in countenance. But what if you were shown each in a separate cage?"

Her face brightened. "Oh, now I understand, Mr. Renwick! You mean it would be nicer for the Editors, too, to be seen all together."

Renwick sighed hopelessly. She spoke on decisively: "That may be a valuable suggestion, Mr. Renwick." On her pad she began pencilling shorthand. "Of course I will credit you with it. Perhaps you do not know that Miss Minnely always pays well for valuable suggestions." She wrote intently, murmuring: "But is it practicable? Let me think. Why, surely practicable! But Miss Minnely will decide. All partitions on the Editorial Flat could be removed! Make it cool as Prize Package or Financial Department!" She looked up from her paper, glowing with enterprise, and pointed her pencil straight at Renwick. "And so impressive!" She swept the pencil in a broad half circle, seeing her picture. "Thirty Editors visible at one comprehensive glance! All so literary, and busy, and intelligent, and cordial! Fine! I take the liberty, temporarily, of calling that a first-class suggestion, Mr. Renwick. It may be worth hundreds to you, if Miss Minnely values it. It may be forcibly felt in the Subscription List—if Miss Minnely approves. It may help to hold many subscribers who try to get away after the first year. I feel almost sure Miss Minnely *will* approve. I am so glad. I thought something important was going to come when Miss Minnely considered your placard so carefully."

"But some of the other Editors may not wish to be exhibited with the whole collection," said Renwick gravely. "For instance, consider Mr. Cummins' literary rank. Would it gratify him to be shown as a mere unit among Editors of lesser dintinction?"

"You are most fore-thoughtful on every point, Mr. Renwick. That is so *fine*. But Mr. Cummins is also most devoted. I feel sure he would cordially yield, if Miss Minnely approved. I presume you will wish me to tell her that you are grateful for her kind message?"

"Cordially grateful seems more fitting. Miss Heartly—and I am —especially for her choice of a deputy."

"Thank you, Mr. Renwick. I will tell her that, too. And may I say that you will be pleased to adopt her suggestion that you discourse a little to visitors, pending possible changes in this Flat, instead of just coming forward and turning around. Literary men are so clever—and— ready." He fleetingly suspected her of derision.

"Please say that I will reflect on Miss Minnely's suggestion with an anxious wish to emulate, so far as my fallen nature will permit, Miss Heartly's beautiful devotion to 'The Blessing's' interests."

"Oh, thank you again, so much, Mr. Renwick." And the fair Priestess of Business bowed graciously in good bye.

III

Renwick sat dazed. From his earliest acquaintance with "The Family Blessing" he had thought of its famous Editress and Sole Proprietress as one "working a graft" on the Plain People by consummate sense of the commercial value of cordial cant. Now he had to conceive of her as perfectly ingenuous. Had she really taken his placard as one written in good faith? He remembered its sentences clearly:

> "When the editor in this compartment is to be exhibited, please notify him by knocking on this door before opening it. He will then rise from his sitting posture, come forward for inspection, and turn slowly around three times if a school teacher, a mother, or a minister of the Gospel be among the visiting subscribers."

Miss Minnely took that for sincere! Renwick began to regard "The Blessing" as an emanation of a soul so simple as to be incapable of recognizing the diabolic element, derision. He was conceiving a tenderness for the honesty which could read his placard as one of sincerity. How blessed must be hearts innocent of mockery! Why should he not gratify them by discoursing to visiting subscribers? The idea tickled his fancy. At least he might amuse himself by writing what would edify Durley's parties if delivered with gravity. He might make material of some of Miss Minnely's voluminous letters of instruction to himself. From his pigeon-hole he drew that file, inspected it rapidly, laughed, and culled as he wrote.

Twenty minutes later he was chuckling over the effusion, after having once read its solemnities aloud to himself.

"Hang me if I don't try it on Durley's next party!" he was telling himself, when pencil tickings, like small woodpecker tappings, came again on his outer door. "Miss Heartly back! I will treat her to it!" and he opened the door, discourse in hand.

There stood the wide, wise-eyed, placid, gray-clad lady!

"I am Miss Minnely, Mr. Renwick. Very pleased to introduce myself to a gentleman whose suggestion has pleased me deeply." Her wooly voice as if steeped in a syrup of cordial powers. Suddenly he knew she had reminded him of Miss Pue's gigantic bronze Beneficence.

"Thank you, Miss Minnely. I feel truly honoured." Renwick, with some concealed trepidation, bowed her to his revolving chair.

"Mr. Renwick." She disposed her amplitude comfortably; then streamed on genially and authoritatively, "You may be gratified to learn that I was pleased—on the whole—by your cordial demeanour while—er—revolving—not long ago—on the occasion of Mr. Durley's last visiting party. Only—you will permit me to say this in all kindness— I did not regard the—the display of—er—form—as precisely *adapted.* Otherwise your appearance, tone, and manner were eminently suitable —indeed such as mark you strongly, Mr. Renwick, as conforming— almost—to my highest ideal for the conduct of Editors of 'The Blessing.' Consequently I deputed Miss Heartly—with a suggestion. She has informed me of your cordial willingness, Mr. Renwick—hence I am here to thank you again—and instruct. Your short discourse to visitors will —let me explain—not only edify, but have the effect of, as it were, obviat- ing any necessity for the—er—revolving—and the display of—er—form. Now, you are doubtless aware that I invariably edit, so to speak, every single thing done on behalf of our precious 'Family Blessing.' For due performance of that paramount duty I must give account hereafter. My peculiar gift is Taste—you will understand that I mention this fact with no more personal vanity that if I mentioned that I have a voice, hands, teeth, or any other endowment from my Creator—*our* Creator, in fact. Taste—true sense of what our subscribers like on their *higher* plane. My great gift must be entitled to direct what we *say* to visitors, just as it directs what 'The Blessing' publishes on its story pages, its editorial columns, its advertisements, letter heads, everything of every kind done in 'The Blessing's' name. I am thorough. And so, Mr. Renwick, I desire to hear your discourse beforehand. What? You have already prepared it? Excellent! Promptitude—there are few greater business virtues! We will immediately use your draft as a basis for further consultation."

So imposing was her amiable demeanour that Renwick had no wish but to comply. He glanced over what he had written, feeling now sure that its mock gravity would seem nowise sardonic to Miss Minnely.

"In preparing these few words," he remarked, "I have borrowed liberally from your notes of instruction to me, Miss Minnely."

"Very judicious. Pray give me the pleasure."

He tendered the draft.

"But no, please *deliver* it." She put away the paper. Suppose me to be a party of our de-ar visiting subscribers. I will stand here, you there. Now do not hesitate to be audible, Mr. Renwick." She beamed as a Brobdignagian child at a new game.

Renwick, quick to all humours, took position, and began with unction: "Dear friends, dear visitors——"

She interrupted amiably:—"De-ar friends, de-ar visitors. Make two syllables of the de-ar. The lingering is cordial in effect. I have observed that carefully—de-ar softens hearts. Dwell on the word—dee-ar—thus you will cause a sense of affectionate regard to cling to visitors' memories of 'The Blessing's' editorial staff. You understand, Mr. Renwick?"

He began again: "De-ar friends, de-ar visitors, de-ar mothers, de-ar teachers," but again she gently expostulated, holding up a fat hand to stop his voice.

"Please, Mr. Renwick—no, I think not—it might seem invidious to discriminate by specifying some before others. All alike are our de-ar friends and visitors."

"De-ar friends, de-ar visitors," Renwick corrected his paper, "I cannot hope to express adequately to you my feelings of delight in being introduced to your notice as a first class general purpose editor, and eminent authority on——"

She graciously interposed:—"It might be well to pencil *this* in, Mr. Renwick, "introduced to you by our de-ar colleague, Mr. Durley, the most experienced of our guides to the "Family Blessing" Building, as general purpose editor, etc.' That would impress, as hinting at our corps of guides, besides uplifting the rank of our valued colleague, Mr. Durley, and by consequence 'The Blessing,' through the respectful mention made of one of our more humble employees. Elevate the lowly, and you elevate all the superior classes—that is a sound American maxim. In business it is by such fine attention to detail that hearts and therefore subscribers are won. But, Mr. Renwick, *nothing* could be better than your 'I cannot hope to express adequately my feelings of delight,' etc.—that signifies cordial emotion—it is very good business, indeed."

Sincerity was unclouded in her gaze. He pencilled in her amendment, and read on:—"and eminent authority on water amusements of a character to build up character in first-class respectable American families."

"Very good—I drilled Mr. Durley in that," she put in complacently.

"Dear friends," he resumed.

"De-ar friends," she reminded him.

"De-ar friends, you may naturally desire to be informed of the nature of the duties of a general purpose editor, therefore——"

"Let me suggest again, Mr. Renwick. Better say 'Dear friends, closely associated with "The Family Blessing," as all must feel who share the privilege of maintaining it, you will naturally desire to be informed,' etc. Don't you agree, Mr. Renwick? It is well to neglect no opportunity for deepening the sense of our de-ar subscribers that the 'Blessing' is a privilege to their households. I do everything possible to make our beloved ones feel that they *own* 'The Blessing,' as in the highest sense they do. They like that. It is remunerative, also."

Renwick jotted in the improvement, and read on: "A general purpose editor of 'The Blessing' is simply one charged with promoting the general purpose of 'The Blessing.' To explain what that is I cannot do better than employ the words of the Sole Proprietress, Miss Minnely herself, and——."

The lady suggested, *"I cannot do so well as to employ the words of* —it is always effective to speak most respectfully of the absent Proprietress—that touches their imagination favourably. It is good business."

"I appreciate it, Miss Minnely. And now I venture to adapt, *verbatim,* parts of your notes to me."

"It was forethoughtful to preserve them, Mr. Renwick. I am cordially pleased."

He read on more oratorically:—"De-ar friends, 'The Blessing' has a Mission, and to fulfil that Mission it must, first of all, entertain its subscribers on their *higher plane.* This cannot be done by stimulating in them any latent taste for coarse and inelegant laughter, but by furnishing entertainingly the wholesome food from which mental pabulum is absorbed and mental growth accomplished."

"Excellent! My very own words."

"The varieties of this entertaining pabulum must be *conscientiously* prepared, and administered in small quantities so that each can be assimilated unconsciously by Youth and Age without mental mastication. Mind is *not* Character, and——"

"How true. Character-building publications must *never* be addressed to mere *Mind."*

"The uplifting of the Mind, or Intellect," Renwick read on, "is not the general purpose of 'The Family Blessing.' It is by the Literature of the Heart that Character is uplifted. Therefore a general purpose editor of 'The Blessing' must ever seek to maintain and to present the *truly cordial.* That is what most widely attracts and pleases all these sections of the great American people who are uncorrupted by worldly and literary associations which tend to canker the Soul with cynicism."

"I remember my glow of heart in writing those inspiring, blessed, and inspired words!" she exclaimed. "Moreover, they are true. Now,

I think that is about enough, Mr. Renwick. Visitors should never be too long detained by a single attraction. Let me advise you to memorize the discourse carefully. It is cordial. It is impressive. It is informative of 'The Blessing's' ideal. It utters my own thoughts in my own language. It is admirably adapted to hold former subscribers, and to confirm new. All is well." She pondered silently a few moments. "Now, Mr. Renwick, I would be strictly just. The fact that an editor, and one of those not long gathered to our happy company, has suggested and devoted himself to this novel attraction, will have noblest effect in rousing our colleagues of every Department to emulative exertion. Once more, I thank you cordially. But the Sole Proprietress of the remunerative 'Blessing' holds her place in trust for all colleagues, and she is not disposed to retire with mere thanks to one who has identified himself so effectually with her and its ideals. Mr. Renwick, your honorarium—your weekly pay envelope," again she paused reflectively, "it will hereafter rank you with our very valued colleague, Mr. Caliphas C. Cummins himself! No—no-no, Mr. Renwick—do not thank me—thank your happy inspira-tion—thank your cordial devotion—thank your *Taste*—thank your natural. innate identification, in high ideals, with me and 'The Family Blessing.' As for me—it is for me to thank you—and I do so, again, cordially, cordially, cordially!" She beamed, the broad embodiment of Beneficence, in going out of the room.

Renwick long stared, as one dazed, at the story of "The Converted Ringmaster." It related in minute detail the sudden reformation of that sinful official. The account of his rapid change seemed no longer improbable nor mawkish. Any revolution in any mind might occur, since his own had been so swiftly hypnotized into sympathy with Miss Minnely and her emanation "The Blessing." How generous she was! Grateful mist was in his eyes, emotion for the safety of the widows and the orphan whose bread he must win.

Yet the derisive demon which sat always close to his too sophisticated heart was already gibing him afresh:—"You stand engaged," it sneered, "as assistant ringmaster to Durley's exhibition of yourself!"

New perception of Miss Minnely and Miss Heartly rose in his mind. Could mortal women be really as simple as those two ladies had seemed? Might it not be they had managed him with an irony as profound as the ingenuousness they had appeared to evince?

THE AUTHOR

Edward William Thomson was born February 12, 1849 on a farm in Toronto township, Peel County, Ontario. His mother, Margaret Hamilton Foley, was the daughter of an Irish family which had come to Canada in 1822. His father, William Thomson, was of Scottish and United Empire Loyalist ancestry.

At the age of fifteen Thomson served briefly with the Union Army in the American Civil War. In 1866 he enlisted in the Queen's Own Rifles and fought against the Fenians at Ridgeway. He studied civil engineering and surveying and worked from 1872 to 1878 as a land surveyor in eastern Ontario. From 1878 to 1891, except for a two year return to surveying in the west in 1882, Thomson was an editorial writer with the Toronto *Globe*. He spent the next ten years in Boston as revising editor of *Youth's Companion*, returning to Canada in 1901. After a year with the Montreal *Star*, he became Canadian correspondent for the *Boston Transcript* and continued in this position until 1922. During these years Thomson lived in Ottawa where he was a close fried of major political and literary figures of that time. He died in Boston in 1924.

SELECTED BIBLIOGRAPHY

WORKS BY EDWARD WILLIAM THOMSON

Old Man Savarin and Other Stories. Toronto: William Briggs, 1895.

Aucussin et Nicolet. Boston: Copeland and Day, 1896.

Smoky Days. New York: Thomas Y. Crowell, 1896.

Walter Gibbs, the Young Boss; and Other Stories. A Book for Boys, Toronto: William Briggs, 1896.

Between Earth and Sky, and Other Strange Stories of Deliverance. Toronto: William Briggs, 1897.

Peter Ottawa. Toronto: Privately printed, 1905.
  This poem is re-published in *The Many Mansioned House and Other Poems.*

The Many Mansioned House and Other Poems. Toronto: William Briggs, 1909.

When Lincoln Died and Other Poems. Boston: Houghton Mifflin Company, 1909. The American edition of *The Many Mansioned House and Other Poems,* with a slight variation in the order of the poems and the omission of two poems "Aspiration" and "The Canadian Abroad".

Old Man Savarin Stories. Tales of Canada and Canadians. Toronto: S.B. Gundy, 1917. Contains twelve of the fourteen stories published in *Old Man Savarin and Other Stories,* with the addition of two stories from *Between Earth and Sky, and Other Strange Stories of Deliverance* and three previously uncollected stories.

92

CRITICAL ARTICLES, LETTERS, AND REVIEWS

BOURINOT, Arthur S. *Edward William Thomson (1849-1924).* A Bibliography with Notes and some Letters. Ottawa: Arthur S. Bourinot, 1955.

—, ed. *Archibald Lampman Letters to Edward William Thomson (1890-1898).* Ottawa: Arthur S. Bourinot, 1956.

—, ed. *The Letters of Edward William Thomson to Archibald Lampman (1891-1897).* Ottawa: Arthur S. Bourinot, 1957.

DEFOE, J.W. "E.W. Thomson: Canadian Journalist and Poet," Literary Section of the *Free Press*, Winnipeg, Monday, April 7, 1924.

HAMMOND, M.O. "Edward William Thomson," *Queen's Quarterly*, 38 (winter 1931), 123-139.

LAMPMAN, Archibald, "Review of Thomson's Old Man Savarin," *The Week*, August 9, 1895.

MacLELLAN, W.E. "Topics of the Day," *Dalhousie Review*, 2 (October 1922), 374-375.

PEACOCK, H.R. "A Biographical and Critical Study of Edward William Thomson," thesis, University of New Brunswick, 1949.